Mrs. Hudson for the Defense

By

Barry S Brown

Paperback ISBN 978-1-80424-465-4
ePub ISBN 978-1-80424-466-1
PDF ISBN 978-1-80424-467-8

Published by MX Publishing
335 Princess Park Manor, Royal Drive,
London, N11 3GX
www.mxpublishing.com

Cover design by Awan

Praise for earlier accounts of Mrs. Hudson's achievements:

"Each new book surpasses the others ... Some enterprising TV producer is missing out on a potentially great TV mystery series!"
Over My Dead Body Mystery Magazine

"... an inherently entertaining and fascinating read from beginning to end ... an enduringly popular addition to community library Mystery/ Suspense collections ..,"
Midwest Book Review

"It is always a pleasure to recommend a Sherlock Holmes novel that retains the reader's interest to the very end. This one did."
Sherlockian.net

"Brown's novels [are] light, swift, and with underlying humor, they make one want to huzzah and call God Save the Queen."
Wilmington Star-News

"enormously entertaining ... the amusingly quirky Mrs. Hudson of Baker Street series in which the formidable landlady proves to be the sage of Baker Street. ... And she still finds the time to make scones (plain and raisin-filled)."
The District Messenger – Newsletter of the Sherlock Holmes Society of London

"... an intriguing narrative ..."
Strand Magazine

And from the author's three children:

"Wasn't bad."

"I've read worse."

"Wait. He writes? Books?"

Mrs. Hudson Adventures

The Unpleasantness at Parkerton Manor

Mrs. Hudson and the Irish Invincibles

Mrs. Hudson in the Ring

Mrs. Hudson in New York

Mrs. Hudson's Olympic Triumph

Mrs. Hudson Takes the Stage

Mrs. Hudson and the Wild West

Mrs. Hudson for the Defense

Dedication

To Rebecca in recognition of her courage and resolve in the face of enormous adversity.

Acknowledgment

I am indebted to Arlyne and Marvin Snyder for their careful review, comment and many suggestions and corrections.
I am indebted as well to Joanna Norland and Alistair McLeod for their efforts to steer me accurately around London's streets.
If, nonetheless, the reader finds him/herself lost due to either misdirection or cumbersome phrasing, the fault is entirely the author's.

Disclaimer

While real people are included in the course of this novel, the activities and ideas ascribed to them are consistent with this being a work of fiction, and can be attributed to the author's overactive imagination.

Chapter 1.
A Fugitive from Justice

If Thomas Wiggins was not the last person Holmes expected to see on the doorstep of his Sussex Downs cottage, he would certainly have ranked high on any such list. The explanation he offered for his unexpected appearance did little to reduce Holmes's confusion.

"You're needed, Mr. Holmes. I'm to bring you to Inspector Lestrade. Dr. Watson has been accused of murder."

Holmes stared a long moment at Wiggins, his eyebrows at full mast, waiting for the grin from the former leader of the Baker Street Irregulars—and sometimes petty thief—that would reveal the prank he was hoping to pull off. His stare was met instead with the blank look of perfect innocence. Holmes recognized that a satisfactory explanation for Wiggins's presence and strange declaration was not to be had, nor were the minimal demands of hospitality to be met, if they remained on his doorstep.

"Perhaps you should come inside, Thomas, and tell me what you know."

Wiggins signaled for the driver of the four-wheeler he had engaged to wait, then turned to enter the door Holmes had thrown wide. Holmes led him to a small parlor where he paused before following Holmes's directive to "have a seat." His uncertainty about which of the three unmatched chairs to select was relieved when Holmes took the rocker for himself and gestured for him to choose the armed easy chair by the still fireplace. Summer had ended the week before and, try as it might, fall had not yet established a presence sufficient to justify even a modest fire.

"Now, what's all this about Watson being seen as a murderer?" Holmes asked.

"It's true, Mr. Holmes. The doctor's brother-in-law is dead, poisoned, and they're saying it's Dr. Watson's doing. I can tell you it's got me and Inspector Lestrade very upset."

Holmes let pass Wiggins's portrayal of an equivalence between himself and his one-time occasional adversary, choosing instead to remain focused on the mystery at hand. He had been gone from the London scene for three years but had remained reasonably well informed of events in the city through the visits of Watson and some few others. Thus, he knew of the death of Margaret Watson, the doctor's second wife, of Lestrade's retirement from the Yard and Wiggins's marriage and not entirely coincidental ascendence to junior printer at Lewin and Sons. Indeed, the "and Sons" had been dropped as neither accurate nor needed any longer to assure the public of the firm's stability. Nonetheless, whatever the change in his circumstances, Holmes could not conceive of Wiggins having attained equal footing with the inspector anywhere other than in Wiggins's fertile imagination. However, Holmes dared not explore any side issue if he was to learn any time soon about Watson's dilemma and his strange alliance with Lestrade.

"Suppose you start at the beginning. Leave nothing out and make clear the inspector's role in all this."

"I'll tell you what I know, Mr. Holmes, but it's not like they took me into their confidence. Mostly, they thought that with you not having a telephone, I could be sent to tell you enough about the problem to get you to come right away. I figure they weren't worried about me being followed since they wouldn't know about our connection." Again, Holmes marveled at the status Thomas Wiggins had achieved in the eyes of Thomas Wiggins. Again, he marveled silently.

"All that I know," Wiggins reported, "is that the trouble started at a dinner party Dr. Watson gave several months after Mrs. Watson died. Lucinda, that's my wife, Mr. Holmes, says it was a kind of memorial that people do for someone who's died. I'm sure that's right 'cause Lucinda knows about those things. I can't wait for you to meet her, Mr. Holmes. She's real smart, smarter than me certainly. Anyway, it was at the party—or memorial—that there was a murder. Mrs. Watson's brother, Reginald Miles, was poisoned and the doctor was seen as the murderer."

Wiggins paused, inhaled deeply and looked to a distant vision only he could see. Holmes prepared himself for a lengthy digression whose emergence appeared to be beyond Wiggins's control.

"I'll tell you, Mr. Holmes, from everything I hear about this Reginald, I could have been him. I was going down the same wrong roads he went down when you, the doctor and Mrs. H took me in to be your page and got me straightened out. Without that, it's for sure I wouldn't be a junior printer learning a trade from a master printer the likes of Mr. Lewin. And I wouldn't of ever met Mr. Lewin's daughter, Lucinda. She's made all the difference you know." Wiggins's far-away look returned, now accompanied by a dreamy smile. The lengthy pause following that smile allowed Holmes to put an end to Wiggins's description of the disaster his life would have been compared to the success he now enjoyed.

"You were telling me about Watson being accused of murdering his brother-in-law." Holmes tried to sound less testy than he felt.

"Yes, I'm sorry, Mr. Holmes. I was just reminded of my own good fortune. Anyway, that's about all there is to tell—or, at least, that's all I know. Except that they put bobbies outside the house to make sure Dr. Watson wasn't going anyplace until the police wagon came to get him in the morning, but he somehow got away from them and went to see Inspector Lestrade. It was after that that the inspector and Dr. Watson got me involved in all that was happening. The inspector got in touch with Mr. Lewin and told him he

3

needed me for an important mission. 'Mission' was the word he used. I remember because it made everything sound real official. I was to go to the address the inspector gave Mr. Lewin, and he was to lose the address and forget he ever got a phone call. I can tell you my father-in-law was very impressed."

Holmes's brow had begun to furrow earlier and the furrows proceeded to deepen as Wiggins continued his narrative. When Wiggins paused again, this time in search of additional details to share, Holmes seized the moment to request clarification of a point he found particularly difficult to process.

"Are you saying that not only is Watson charged with a crime he obviously could not have committed, but that Lestrade has offered Watson his home to avoid capture by the police? Am I to understand that the two of them are now working together to prove Watson's innocence?"

"It didn't seem natural to me either, Mr. Holmes, and I asked Dr. Watson how it all happened when I got a chance to be alone with him after the inspector was out of the room. To tell you the truth, I also wanted to know how he managed such a smooth getaway from the bobbies that was supposed to be watching him.

"Well, to hear him tell it, getting away from the bobbies was the easiest thing in the world. See, it was late by the time they finally caught up with the doctor, and it didn't seem like he was going anyplace that night, so instead of taking him down to the station and filling out a whole lot of forms that would take half the night, they left him in his own house with one constable at his front door and another at his back door. Well, you can bet they won't be doing that again any time soon.

"The first thing Dr. Watson did when he was alone in the house was to call Inspector Lestrade for advice. He said he knew the inspector wouldn't think he was a murderer, and what with him being retired from the Yard, he could talk to the inspector without anybody getting in trouble. Well, that's when Dr. Watson got what he called the surprise of his life. The inspector asked him where the constables were stationed. When he heard they were front and back, he told the doctor that if he could get away out a side window when it got really dark, he should make for the nearest hotel, hire a coach from one of those lined up in front and take it to— and he gave him an address that turned out to be two streets from where the inspector lived—which was an address he also gave Dr. Watson for him to use as soon as the coach was out of sight. He told him Mrs. Lestrade was away visiting her mother, so they'd have the house to themselves. Which Dr. Watson never expected, and which was what he called the big surprise."

Wiggins paused and pointed to his throat, at the same time looking as piteous as he could manage. "My throat's that dry, Mr. Holmes. Could I trouble you for a drink of water, please?"

Wiggins pretended not to see Holmes's pursed lips and hard squint as he went wordlessly to the adjoining kitchen to return shortly thereafter, water glass in hand, pursed lips and hard squint still intact. Holmes waited for the glass to be emptied and a lengthy sigh of satisfaction to be emitted before calling on Wiggins to return to his narrative.

Cradling the empty glass on his lap, Wiggins acknowledged Holmes's request with a brief nod before resuming.

"There is one more thing you should know. Well, maybe two. The first is something I overheard Dr. Watson say to Inspector Lestrade when he thought I had already left the room. It's something he called 'real worrying.' He said that before he died, this Reginald Miles accused Dr. Watson of killing him, and he believes that everybody who was at the dinner would've heard him say it.

5

"The second thing is more just curious. Dr. Watson insisted that, in addition to my coming to get you, Inspector Lestrade was to get in touch with Mrs. H and let her know about the goings-on. He seemed to have his mind set on that. Except what I know, and they don't, is that if Mrs. H is to be a part of all this, somebody will first have to get her out of jail."

Holmes decided there had been enough surprises for the moment and if they were to get to Lestrade's at a reasonable hour, he would need to defer to later learning how the second of his fellow residents at 221B had also managed to put herself at odds with the law. He threw together clothes and toiletries that he thought would be sufficient for the several days he believed it might take to establish Watson's innocence, then carefully filled a second Gladstone bag with the makeup and materials that would allow for whatever disguises the investigation might require, even as it would supplement the makeup secreted in the armoire in his former bedchamber at 221B.

With a hastily scrawled note for his housekeeper, and a nod to Wiggins signifying his readiness, Holmes strolled to the coach under the critical gaze of its driver who had been patiently calculating what fee he could reasonably charge for the time spent outside Holmes's cottage waiting to be joined by his passengers.

Once comfortably settled in their compartment on the London, Brighton, and South Coast Railway, Holmes posed the question he had earlier put off asking. "You said Mrs. Hudson was taken to jail. Was she also accused of murdering someone?" he asked hopefully.

Wiggins stared open-mouthed at Holmes a moment before giving way to the peals of laughter he thought certain Holmes intended with his question. Collecting himself, he quickly dashed whatever hopes lay behind the question.

"Nothing like that, Mr. Holmes." Then, after pausing to allow two men to pass beyond hearing, he leaned in close to Holmes, and speaking just above a whisper, he asked, "Are you aware that some women have been after getting themselves the vote?"

"Yes, of course, I'd heard about that. The news does reach us even in far off Sussex. What has that to do with Mrs. Hudson?"

After a look toward the now vacant aisle, Wiggins gave voice to his shocking news, "She's one of them." He nodded affirmation of himself, then sat back and waited Holmes's stunned response. When he got none, he decided to elaborate.

"She was marching with them—that's pretty much what they do, march—when, all of a sudden, things went crosswise. Some people threw stones, breaking some windows, and that got the bobbies to rounding up marchers and hauling them off to Bow Street and other stations. Mrs. H was one of the people who got rounded up. That's something Doctor Watson and the inspector don't know. The only reason I know is because Lucinda was one of them, too—a marcher, I mean. She swears she wasn't throwing any rocks and I'm sure neither was Mrs. H. Anyway, Lucinda got away somehow." Wiggins again looked to the empty aisle before continuing.

"All that has got to stay secret, Mr. Holmes. Her father would have a fit if he found out about her taking part, and Mr. Lewin wouldn't be too pleased with me for letting her join the march—as if I could stop her."

By the end of Wiggins's narrative Holmes was grinning broadly. Wiggins assumed Holmes found amusing his report of the conflict within the Lewin family. In fact, Holmes's amusement had nothing to do with the Lewins and everything to do with the image of Mrs. Hudson's arrival at the Bow Street station. The grin softened over time, but its ghost lingered all the way to Victoria Station.

The row of terraced housing within which Inspector Lestrade's home stood was unlike any Holmes had ever seen, and Wiggins made no effort to hide a broad grin on seeing Holmes's obvious astonishment as he exited the four-wheeler they'd taken from the station. No house was painted the same color as the ones adjoining. In blocks of four, houses were painted in pale shades of blue, red, yellow, or green, the pattern repeating itself through the sixteen attached houses. Each house had a privacy wall at the edge of its property that ran parallel to the adjoining sidewalk. The wall's height of less than three feet precluded its providing privacy from the prying eyes of anyone aged four or greater. Wiggins pointed Holmes in the direction of a house in green with a small garden plot containing a colorful mix of peony, hollyhocks, lavender, and foxglove, all planted in a somewhat haphazard, but nonetheless attractive arrangement. The house itself seemed to have been set out in two stages. An initial section showed a large bay window on the ground floor and two windows on the landing above. A second section, recessed several feet back from the first and less than half its width, contained an entry door on its ground floor and a single window on the landing above. All the windows had thin frames of pale green, maintaining the designer's unrelenting commitment to a one-color scheme for each house. Only the oaken paneled entry door deviated from that pattern.

Wiggins knocked three times in rapid succession, then a fourth time after a short pause. Responding to the code they'd developed, Lestrade opened the door to admit his two visitors. He gave Holmes a brief nod and the smallest part of a smile after first looking to the empty street beyond. Holmes followed Lestrade into the parlor. It was only then that Lestrade welcomed Holmes to his home with words of near cordiality, a welcoming that was all but ignored by Holmes when he laid eyes on Watson. He was unable to hide his alarm as he greeted his old friend. Pockets under Watson's eyes were matched by worry lines that had the effect of ageing his friend well beyond the time since they'd last seen each other. Grasping the doctor's hand in both of his, Holmes tried to provide the reassurance both men needed.

"Watson, I can see this experience has taken a terrible toll on you, as it would on any man wrongfully accused of such a crime. Let me assure you everything will be done to get to the bottom of this and set things right, just as we have done so many times before."

Watson forced a near smile in deference to his friend, and Lestrade did his best to sound an optimistic note of his own. "There's no question–none at all–that with Mr. Holmes on the case we can, and we will get this properly sorted."

Holmes turned in response to the voice behind him and for the first time took note of the change in Lestrade's appearance. There was still the sallow cast to his features, but the furtive look had given way to one more brooding, and there now was added—or subtracted as the case might be—a receding hairline countered, with mixed success at best, by what appeared to be a newly grown and still somewhat patchy beard.

Holmes made no comment about the change in appearance and instead spoke to Lestrade with unaccustomed warmth. "This is a wonderful thing you're doing, Inspector. I'm sure my friend has already expressed his profound gratitude to you. I am only troubled about the response of your good wife to visitors—especially given the circumstances of Watson's visit. I understand she's away currently but I'm wondering when she'll be back."

"My wife is visiting her mother in Bristol and won't be back for another week, Mr. Holmes. There could be a problem with my son or daughter, although it seems unlikely.

Noah has a flat in Chelsea and between his job and one thing and another, he's unlikely to pay me a visit until his mother gets back; and Millicent is having too much fun with the girl friends she's moved in with to pay any great mind to her father." Lestrade accompanied what might have been a critical comment with a wry grin that made clear his understanding, if not support, for his daughter's strike for independence and the good times that independence promised. "One thing you should know, Mr. Holmes. My son has decided to follow in his father's footsteps and is a constable with the Metropolitan Police Force. As you can guess, it will not help his career if his father is found to be harboring a fugitive—begging your pardon, Dr. Watson."

Watson waved away any reason to take umbrage, at the same time suggesting a course of action that he hoped would start them on a path to prove his innocence. "Inspector, perhaps this is a good time to make Holmes current with my situation."

As he had hoped, his words were taken as a signal to seat themselves and await a review of the events leading up to his brother-in-law's death. Wiggins, concerned that he might be asked to leave if he did not act swiftly, staked out a ladderback chair near to where he was standing beside the door. It allowed him to remain a party to the investigation, although a somewhat distant and mildly uncomfortable party.

After first assessing the seating options available, Holmes and Watson tacitly agreed on the pale blue cushioned settee, leading Lestrade to choose the spacious Morris chair that faced the two of them across a low table, bare except for a Chinese vase purposely set just slightly off-center. He looked critically to Wiggins off to his left but decided to accept his presence as established fact, as Wiggins hoped he would. To ensure the legitimacy of his continuing presence, Wiggins pulled some sheets of paper from a jacket pocket, a pencil from another and pledged to take notes, while acknowledging that he was, however, "no Dr. Watson."

With a brief nod to the inspector, and a briefer one still to Wiggins, the man who was Dr. Watson focused his attention almost wholly on Holmes as he began the report of his having become a wanted man. "You'll remember, Holmes, that shortly after you left 221B to take up beekeeping, I married a second time, a woman named Margaret Castleton, a widow whose maiden name was Miles. Of course, I had left Baker Street as well and, at Margaret's request, I moved into her home where, she said, she would be near family and friends and feel the most comfortable. Indeed, the people who were at the dinner party were all people known to Margaret for many years, although there were some she hadn't seen in a good long time. Speaking of which, Holmes, we always planned to have you over so the two of you could get to know each other, but somehow we were never able to make it happen. I'll always regret that." Watson swallowed hard before continuing.

"Margaret was a lovely woman. Perhaps a trifle young for me—I know that's what people said—but I was terribly lonely after Mary died, and your move to Sussex simply exacerbated an already difficult situation. You'll remember I always envied your ability to live alone. Anyway, Margaret was lonely as well is the truth of it. She'd lost her husband to typhoid after a long and difficult illness, and we drew comfort from each other. At least we did until her own terribly untimely death." Watson paused a moment as if to catch his breath, everyone aware the pause was not solely to catch his breath.

"Before she died, Margaret asked me to promise I would do what I could for her brother, Reginald, who was frankly a ne'er-do-well—worse than that, really. He seemed to care little about anyone but himself and treated those around him with near contempt. His penchant for gambling had long since driven away his wife and son. She had remarried and would have nothing to do with him. His son, Reginald Junior, routinely asked people to call him by his middle name, Edward, which tells you something of his feelings for his father.

"Margaret never saw that, almost certainly because she was the one person he took care to avoid alienating. In any event, when she knew she was dying, she asked me to do what I could to reacquaint him with the respectable friends he once had, it being her opinion that it was his more recent companions who had led him astray. To that end she prepared a list for me consisting of the people she deemed respectable, and that she believed had once been close to Reginald, some of whom she thought might still be, or might become so again.

"Margaret, you must know, was as much beloved as her brother was not and so, after a suitable period of mourning, I invited the people on her list to our home for dinner and to pay their respects to Margaret. I also took the precaution of giving the Smythes, John and Clara, Margaret's long-time and very loyal cook and butler, the evening off. It's been my experience that people don't speak as freely as they might when servants are going in and out. Moreover, it was my understanding there was no love lost between the Smythes and Reginald and I saw no reason to expose either to needless difficulty. Anyway, I had Clara do a roast and set it warming in the oven and assured John I'd take care of the serving.

"When all was set in place, I thought there was at least a chance Reginald would not be the Reginald of old and those who had known him might, as Margaret hoped, give him a second chance. And, at least early on in the evening, everyone was at pains to be civil to Reginald, and Reginald was restrained in return—largely, I would have to say, by saying little through much of the dinner.

"In any event, there came a point at which things started to go downhill as people exhausted reminiscences of Margaret and began to share reminisces of Reginald. It started in a light vein, one person recalling Reginald as quite the ladies' man, leading another to note under his breath, but a little too loudly, that the marital state of his ladies was not always of concern to Reginald. Someone else remembered Reginald's good business practices, but then, as examples were cited, 'good' became 'sharp' and sharp turned into 'shady.'

"And I have to say, even with that Reginald remained under good self-control. The only person he turned on was me and, on that score, he was quite harsh, accusing me of not taking care of Margaret as I should have, and some things worse than that that were pretty despicable. He even claimed that Margaret complained to him about my behavior—which I'm certain was a bald-faced lie. I was about ready to call the evening at an end when Reginald's son, Edward, suggested we all move to my study before having dessert to allow me to share the photographs I'd taken of our trip to the Highlands, which, as things turned out, was our last trip before Margaret became ill. Edward and his wife, Alice, had seen the photographs on a visit to us, but no one else had. Between the unpleasantries starting to invade the dinner conversation and the pride I take in my new hobby, I readily agreed with the suggestion. As it turned out, everyone thought it would be a good idea to take some time before dessert, I suspect less to see my photographs than to let things quiet down.

"In any event, with help from some of the guests, I cleared the dinner plates and glasses, then excused my helpers from any further work and by myself, set out dessert plates, as well as glasses for port. Although I couldn't have known it at the time, it proved to be a great mistake for me to do things out of sight of everyone.

"In terms of the glasses for port, there were, in fact, two mistakes. The first was, as I've said, putting them out by myself leading people—anyway, some people—to say later that I had opportunity to put cyanide in Reginald's glass without being seen. The second, was to choose to use our frosted glasses rather than the clear. It is, of course, harder to see what's in frosted glasses, so my choice could be seen as motivated by something other than a wish to set out the more attractive of the two sets of dessert wine glasses—which, of course, was my sole purpose.

"There was one other time I was alone in the dining room. At one point I broke off showing the photographs long enough to check on things in the kitchen. With the Smythes not there, I wanted to make sure the roast looked like I thought it should look. Of course, I went through the dining room and passed everyone's place settings to get to the kitchen. You should understand I was far from the only one who left the study. I didn't keep track, but it seemed to me almost everyone, if not everyone, left the room at one time or another. I heard someone say he—it was a man's voice—wanted to get some air, another volunteered to go outside to smoke 'so as not to offend the ladies.' There were a number who mumbled their excuse me's who I assume were wanting to use the facilities. I could tell you who at least some of them were, but the truth is there were some I was meeting for the first time and wouldn't have recognized their voices under the best of circumstances. And, of course, it wasn't the best of circumstances because I was intent on being the good host in terms of explaining about each photograph and barely took note of those comings and goings. Of course, I had no idea how important that would be; nonetheless, I'm sorry I wasn't more observant."

For his part, Holmes brushed away any unease about the lack of information both knew to be critical. "It's of no concern, Watson, there'll be a host of clues, I'm sure, once we begin our investigation."

Watson's look made clear there was something more he felt obliged to share and, after first clearing his throat twice, he revealed what it was. "There is something else that you should know. I was very angry with Reginald after Margaret died. He had continued to make selfish demands on her, even when he knew she was dying, and it seemed to me he barely shed a tear at her passing. It all just got to me and I'm afraid I told some people how I felt, including that I held him partly responsible for her death. It was said in the heat of the moment—although I take none of it back. In any event, I'm sure it had come to be known by everyone at the table, including Reginald, of course. Maybe that's why he looked at me with daggers a good part of the evening and, while he tried to be civil with all the others, it was almost as if he was trying to goad me into a fight with him as I'm sure everyone who was there would tell you.

"I'll give just one example of what was going on. When we had all reassembled in the dining room, I thought I should refill everyone's water glass. I got halfway round to where Reginald was sitting and picked up his glass to pour when he decided he didn't need his glass filled and tried to grab it back from me, but it was slippery and my hand was wet, and the glass fell to the floor and broke into several pieces. Reginald claimed quite loudly that it was all my fault, and I was purposely trying to embarrass him or maybe do worse. It was quite silly really but indicated his feelings toward me. He then insisted on picking up the pieces of glass himself, claiming I would cut him in another supposed accident if I handled the pieces of glass with him. Well, upset as he was, the inevitable happened and he managed to get a good size laceration on his hand. Of course, I offered to clean it out and bandage it, but he quite loudly rejected any help from me, insisting that I stay away from him, that he didn't trust me to do anything for him. Instead, he pulled out a handkerchief which he asked Alice, his daughter-in-law, to help him make into a bandage. Apart from how unhygienic that was, it didn't adequately cover the cut and he removed it altogether a short time later when the bleeding seemed to have stopped. His words were very likely a shock reaction to the wound he had suffered. Nonetheless, I'm certain it had an unfortunate influence on how people saw things—saw me— a short time later.

"Anyway, when we were all back at the table, I filled the glasses with port. After which someone proposed a toast to Margaret, which, of course, had to be honored. We all stood and drank our glasses and, immediately after, Reginald fell back in his chair, clutching his throat and moaning hoarsely. With great effort, he pulled himself up to a near standing position, pointed in my direction, said the one word, 'You,' and fell dead across the table. Well, of course, that one word, taken with all that had gone before, sealed my fate, first with my guests and later with the police—and I can't say I blame them for thinking as they did, except, of course, I didn't kill Reginald. I knew right away it was almost certainly cyanide to work that quickly. But I can't understand how it could get into Reginald's glass and no other.

"Regardless, all of that led to my making use of a side window in my home to get away from my captors and coming to rely on the courage and good heartedness of Inspector Lestrade." As Watson's voice dropped, there was a cough followed by throat clearing from the ladderback chair, the sounds causing Watson to amend his comment about the people to whom he was indebted.

"And, of course, there was the important contribution of Mr. Thomas Wiggins."

The cough now under control, its owner added, "And Lucinda. Not with Dr. Watson exactly but in a way that's connected. See, Lucinda took care of things at Baker Street after Mrs. H got arrested." Wiggins looked to each member of his audience, satisfying himself he had their full, if bemused, attention.

"What happened was Lucinda met up with Mrs. H at the women's march for votes. Of course, that wasn't the first time they met. Mrs. H actually first got to meet Lucinda at our wedding, but that wasn't much more than to say 'hello.' They had more of a sit-down talk when I brought Lucinda by 221B a few months after. Of course, by that time Mr. Holmes was in Sussex and Dr. Watson was gone as well. Anyway, when they recognized each other at the march, and Mrs. H felt comfortable enough with Lucinda that when she saw she wasn't going to be able to avoid getting arrested, she slipped her the keys to 221B and asked her to watch over things until she got back which, of course, Lucinda agreed to do.

"But there's more. Before going to get Mr. Holmes, Lucinda told me Mrs. H has been let go by the police and is now back to 221B. Mrs. H wanted Lucinda to let us know she's staying put right now because she thinks if she goes anyplace, she'll have the police for company in hopes of her leading them to Dr. Watson." Wiggins again looked to each member of his audience, now with a satisfied smile and a shirtfront that seemed to threaten to pop a button or two in the wake of gaining recognition for his and Lucinda's accomplishments. And, as he had promised Lucinda, he had not revealed the most extraordinary part of the story as it involved Mrs. H and Lucinda, a part that would have to be revealed to Mr. Holmes before he got back to Baker Street.

Chapter 2.
No One Is Quite Who They Seem

Constable Chase had insisted on driving Mrs. Hudson home in the four-wheeler he borrowed for the occasion, all the while making repeated apologies for what he described as "a dreadful error, treating you like you was a common criminal and leaving you to spend the night with the likes of London's worst element for company."

Mrs. Hudson felt it would be inappropriate to inform the constable that she found the whole experience educational and strangely exhilarating. Instead, she expressed appreciation for his understanding, assured him she was "just fine," and thanked him repeatedly for getting her home.

Lucinda was at the door of 221B as Constable Chase, taking no chance of Mrs. Hudson being waylaid along the path from the four-wheeler to her home, accompanied her as far as her door. Waiting on the doorstep, Lucinda seemed poised to embrace Mrs. Hudson, only recognizing at the last that Mrs. Hudson was not a hugger as she swept past her into the hallway. Nonetheless, the warm smile Mrs. Hudson shared with Lucinda made clear her feelings for the young woman who had lately become her co-conspirator.

"I see the police 'ave been 'ere," Mrs. Hudson said as she looked to her bedroom before turning to enter the parlor.

Mrs. Hudson responded to Lucinda's raised eyebrows without waiting for the question that triggered their ascendance. "The coverlet is part way up from where one of them would have looked under the bed, and the doors to the armoire aren't closed tightly the way I left them." Without waiting for Lucinda's expression to clear, Mrs. Hudson went on to her major concern.

"I take it our little scheme worked."

The grin that now wreathed Lucinda's face confirmed Mrs. Hudson's judgment. "It worked perfectly, Mrs. Hudson. The police came looking for a man, and so they simply ignored two women. And what with the two of them wearing gray wigs, like they were old ..." Lucinda stopped in her recitation, blushing as she did before blurting out an apology. "I'm sorry, Mrs. Hudson, I don't mean you, of course."

The return of Mrs. Hudson's warm smile was as reassuring as her words. "Don't give it a thought. Of course, to a young person such as yourself, I'm an ol ... elderly woman. I understand that. But tell me more about the police visit."

"Both Miss Pankhurst and Miss Kenney took the bedrooms off of the sitting room upstairs. They made themselves up with wigs and lines they put on their faces using pencils they found in what must have been Mr. Holmes's closet. Then, they put stuffing in their clothes to make them look a lot heavier than they really are. I don't think their own mothers would have recognized them after all that. Anyway, between their disguises and the police concern with finding Dr. Watson, everything worked out just like Mr. Holmes would have planned it." Mrs. Hudson winced slightly while Lucinda smiled brightly at her recollection of recent events. Her smile faded and her voice became confidential as the young woman confessed what else she'd done.

"I also felt I had to tell Miss Pankhurst and Miss Kenney what the situation was with Dr. Watson. I'm sorry, Mrs. Hudson, it bothered me to keep them from knowing all they were getting themselves into. I also told them we all believe Dr. Watson is completely innocent and Mr. Holmes will be working to prove that."

To Lucinda's great relief, Mrs. Hudson responded to her confession with several small nods and another big smile.

"It was absolutely the right thing to do what with the police certain to come 'ere lookin' for Dr. Watson. I'm just glad that everythin' worked out so well. You can never be exactly sure what will 'appen when you start pretendin' to be someone you're not. It's a lucky thing Mr. 'Olmes left so much of 'is play-actin' things 'ere." The rustle of skirts on the landing above caused Mrs. Hudson to refocus the conversation. "And now, I could do with a cup of tea and maybe a scone. There's some that's a day old but still better than anythin' I was likely to get at Bow Street. Perhaps our guests would like some tea as well."

The guests in question, now poised at the top of the stairs, answered emphatically in the affirmative as they descended from where they'd been eavesdropping on the exchange below. The nearer of the two called out their names and a greeting as they joined Mrs. Hudson.

"Mrs. Hudson, I'm Christabel Pankhurst and this is my friend, Annie Kenney. We barely got a chance to be introduced at the march what with all that was happening. But I want to thank you now for your kindness and wise planning. We are deeply in yours and Mrs. Wiggins's debt for rescuing us from the police and allowing us to stay at your lodgings house. I believe the correct phrase is 'hiding us out.'" Both women smiled their recognition of the jargon of an underworld with which they had only recently, if nonetheless enthusiastically, affiliated themselves.

Mrs. Hudson showed a faint smile acknowledging the humor they found in a situation she found humorless. She ushered the two women into her parlor where they joined Lucinda, selecting for themselves the settee and the capacity thereby to stay together. Mrs. Hudson judged them to be nearly as young as Lucinda, probably in their mid-twenties, an age when most of their peers would be married and have started a family. Nor, she judged would the women have lacked for suitors had that been their objective.

20

Annie Kenney had a rather long face whose dominant feature was large piercing eyes; Christabel Pankhurst's round face was dominated by soulful, sad eyes that seemed exactly appropriate to her concern for social justice. Both women wore their hair in the same fashionable style of the day, parted in the middle with great waves of hair on either side and puffed rolls of hair behind. Beyond that, and their trim figures, Mrs. Hudson saw the two women as having come together from strikingly different backgrounds. Christabel Pankhurst's dress was of the latest style and fit her as perfectly as an experienced seamstress could manage. Annie Kenney's clothing was less stylish and clung to her just a bit in some places and was just a bit loose in others, as would have been the case with a store-bought dress that lacked the advantage of a seamstress' careful attention. When Mrs. Hudson took the outstretched hands of each woman in greetings, the differences in backgrounds became clearer still.

Christabel Pankhurst's well-manicured hand was without blemish; Annie Kenney's hand showed the nicks and small scars that Mrs. Hudson knew to be the residue of a childhood spent working in a cotton mill. And if the nicks and scars were not sufficient to mark Annie Kenney as a "mill girl," Mrs. Hudson could see that the top two joints of a finger on her right hand were missing, likely lost in an unsuccessful attempt to rethread the bobbin on a sewing machine, a mill task seen as fit for a child worker.

And still, if differences in background and social class were evident to Mrs. Hudson, it was evident as well that the women shared a devotion to their cause that transcended class distinctions. With frequent nods of approval, one for the other, the women routinely expanded on each other's comments, and interrupted each other to drive home a particular point or to highlight an issue, without causing the least upset in the person interrupted. And both revealed the same barely hidden fires when talk turned to women's suffrage and the rights of women. All else apart, the Cause was the great equalizer.

With cups of tea filled, drunk and refilled, and day-old scones consumed by her guests with greater relish than she thought they merited, the conversation turned to the two women's fugitive status.

"I fear we've imposed overlong on your hospitality and kindness, Mrs. Hudson," Christabel Pankhurst began.

"Quite apart from the difficulties our discovery could hold for you and Mrs. Wiggins," added Annie Kenney.

At the mention of her name, Lucinda Wiggins gave her head a vigorous shake. "I'm not concerned about any such difficulties. Are you, Mrs. Hudson?"

"I think we're all quite safe for now." Mrs. Hudson smiled her support for Lucinda. "The police have conducted a thorough search of the buildin' like you'd expect them to and are unlikely to be back for any further visit any time soon. Moreover, at least for now they're lookin' for Dr. Watson, not two suffragettes. Still, our guests 'ave it right, they can't stay 'ere forever." Mrs. Hudson looked to each in turn as she spoke. "Do you 'ave any suitable place to stay?"

The women looked to each other, affected identical grimaces and shook their heads. "If they truly regard us as fugitives from the law," Annie said, "they will be watching our homes and those of our friends and colleagues in the Union."

Christabel elaborated on the comment of her friend and colleague. "We're not a secret organization, Mrs. Hudson. Quite the reverse. We wanted the Women's Social and Political Union to be open to all. And you should know our tactics have changed over time as we've found an appeal to men's better nature to be terribly ineffective. Many of us believe that requests have to give way to demands, and that attacks on property provide an opportunity to make clear our commitment and capacity to make demands. Nonetheless, this was not an instance in which Annie and I took a hand in whatever attacks on property occurred. Indeed, we both saw two constables separate themselves from the other police and begin to throw rocks they appeared to have brought with them. We were near enough to the rock-throwers to give other officers license to arrest us and accuse us of the crime their fellow officers had committed."

Mrs. Hudson pursed her lips as she prepared to share additional bad news with her guests. "Like we've said, the police won't be back for a search anytime soon, but you should know the police have already got a man across the way keepin' a close watch on this building in case Dr. Watson decides to come 'ere. But sooner or later it won't be just Dr. Watson they'll be lookin' for. There's the two of you besides. And just maybe our friend across the roadway recalls or learns that I was at the march and puts that together with the police seein' two unattached ladies roomin' with me when they came lookin' for Dr. Watson. I think we've got to be ready for our friend, or whomever 'e reports to, beginnin' to figure things out. In any event, we've got to plan for the possibility of somethin' like that 'appenin'. That means we've got to get the two of you out of 'ere, only you're sayin' there's nowhere safe for you to go."

Christabel set her jaw before suggesting a course of action that had the sound of an innocent question. "I wonder if your Mr. Holmes wouldn't have some ideas about resolving our troubles. I know he's very involved in helping Dr. Watson—and understandably so—but he might be willing to take a moment for us." She didn't add what was understood—if you'd ask him, Mrs. Hudson.

The mention of Holmes's name triggered a point Annie Kenney thought it important to emphasize in any conversation with the great detective. "He should know it's as Christabel says. We did not throw rocks on this occasion.

I'm not saying we haven't done at some times in the past, but this time it was people who wanted to make us and the movement look bad."

Mrs. Hudson nodded her understanding. "I will certainly tell that to Mr. 'Olmes, and I will, as you suggest, talk to 'im about a plan for resolvin' your difficulties." Mrs. Hudson did not share with them that she already had in mind the strategy that would, in due course, become the one Mr. Holmes would be seen as having created.

"But first, it might be a good idea to get someone in the 'ouse who 'asn't broken any laws—at least for a while—and can come and go without bein' stopped or questioned.

"Lucinda, I'm thinkin' Thomas is about as close to such a person as we can get. 'E will be back to the shop by now. I'd like you to call 'im and ask 'im to come and be with us as soon as possible. Tell 'im not to look across the roadway, but 'e should be aware there'll be someone there watchin' 'is every move. When 'e gets 'ere, you'll answer the door, Lucinda, and after you throw it wide, I want you to give 'im a great big embrace so it's lookin' to the man across the roadway like nothin' more than a boy and a girl glad to see each other."

Lucinda smiled her promise to do as Mrs. Hudson requested while Christabel and Annie reacted with surprise and some confusion to the woman they viewed as Sherlock Holmes's housekeeper unexpectedly making careful observations and directing future action.

Mrs. Hudson did what she could to reduce their surprise and confusion, in the process getting unforeseen assistance from Lucinda. "It's nothin' but the little tricks I learned just by watchin' Mr. 'Olmes all these years. It can't 'elp but make you smarter about people and things."

"That's just what my Tommy says, Mrs. Hudson. He was most impressed with how you picked up on things when he was a page for you all." The slow nods and stony expressions that followed Lucinda's comment gave Mrs. Hudson to understand the two women were satisfied with her explanation but just barely and that it would be well to move things along.

"Lucinda, you need to call Thomas, and don't forget the embrace in the doorway." Lucinda's broad smile made clear it was unlikely she'd forget.

Lucinda went to make her call on the telephone that had only recently been installed and Mrs. Hudson began taking dishes from the parlor to the tub in her kitchen. Christabel and Annie took the unsubtle hint and excused themselves to go back upstairs. When Lucinda had finished her call and taken her smile from the phone in the kitchen to a seat in the parlor, Mrs. Hudson closed the pocket doors separating the two rooms, and called Inspector Lestrade's home, asking to speak to "Mr. 'Olmes."

Had there been an observer, and had that observer been able to see around the back she presented to those beyond the pocket doors, that person would have noted that, in the course of a conversation she appeared to dominate, Mrs. Hudson rarely lost her grimace. Had that same observer been able to piece together the gist of Mrs. Hudson's somewhat muffled speech, it would have become apparent that Mrs. Hudson was not only informing Holmes of the presence of the suffragettes at 221B, but was proposing the strategy Holmes was to follow—and convince Lestrade to follow—in order to move the women from 221B, and, in a larger sense, to keep both Watson and the suffragettes from discovery. If necessary, she told him, he could, this one time, tell Lestrade that the action he proposed was essential to calm the fears of his deeply troubled landlady. Holmes assured Mrs. Hudson he would use his best judgment in deciding how far to go in that regard. In the time it took Holmes to replace the receiver on the call box, Holmes had already decided to take the planned action a considerable distance.

Mrs. Hudson emerged from the kitchen with a forced smile and a brief statement that she was well satisfied with Mr. 'Olmes's plans. Taking her cue from Mrs. Hudson, Lucinda nodded her satisfaction with a plan she was yet to hear, while Christabel and Annie, who had crept back downstairs, only looked questioningly to Mrs. Hudson as they waited to be told what the next disruption to their lives would be. What they heard did not leave them feeling as well satisfied as Mrs. Hudson claimed herself to be, but each declared her willingness to "follow Mr. Holmes's plan."

Thomas Wiggins lost no time getting to 221B where, after first positioning himself in the lodgings house doorway, he gave Lucinda the promised big hug, then improvised a lengthy kiss. He stood, ready to repeat the action, until Mrs. Hudson, noting the inattention of their observer across the roadway, told him it was unnecessary. After shutting the door on his performance, Mrs. Hudson asked him to make a list of four friends who would be willing to work with him for two or more hours and could be trusted to keep a confidence—to the grave if necessary. In return, there would be three shillings, six pence for each man, the sum having been whittled down from the five shillings Wiggins had proposed. Wiggins informed Mrs. Hudson that, as requested, four reliable men (consistent with his new life, he could no longer describe them as friends) would meet at designated points near to, but not in front of Lestrade's home at eleven the next morning. He assured her they were trustworthy; he thought of saying they would be even more trustworthy for an additional shilling each but decided it might be counterproductive to suggest the current sum could prove unequal to the task of buying their silence. At noon, the four men would, with one addition, board carriages for Baker Street.

At noon on that same day, the first of two carriages left 221B headed for the Lestrade home. The second would follow a half hour later, each carriage carrying a young woman artfully transformed into a matronly version of herself. As Mrs. Hudson expected, the man across the roadway paid them no mind, given their resemblance to the description he'd been given of the two women boarding at 221B, and their lack of resemblance to the description that had been circulated of two suffragette lawbreakers. Within that same timeframe two carriages left from a street above the Lestrades' house headed for Baker Street. Only one passenger was aware that one set of travelers was in the process of changing places with the other.

Dr. Watson, who was that passenger, found himself seated beside one of Wiggins's recruits and opposite another. Nor did he look out of place in their company—at least not unless one looked more closely than anyone was likely to. Under the watchful eye of Holmes and the bemused eye of Lestrade, Watson had cleared the grey from his temples, then added a workman's cap that fit snugly over the newly brown coloring he had acquired. He refused, however, to shave the moustache Holmes described as belonging to a prosperous older man—Watson pointing out to Holmes that he was, in fact, a prosperous older man. Holmes then insisted on the addition of a short, scruffy beard and hangdog moustaches to mask that prosperity, "Or," he said, throwing up his hands in what Watson felt to be a needlessly dramatic gesture, "I give up on the whole thing." As a result, Watson had come to be largely indistinguishable from his companions, which he found a decidedly mixed blessing.

Other than a tentative smile there was no communication directed to Watson by his fellow passengers, nor did Watson feel the need to initiate any. Having received the sums negotiated on their behalf by Wiggins, Watson's companions for the afternoon were content to let the next two hours play out while looking ahead to the time they would be free to spend their newly acquired largesse.

As the two carriages containing Wiggins's one-time friends arrived at Baker Street, the sentry across the roadway briefly abandoned his appreciation of the elegant footwear displayed in the window of Farabee's Fine Leather Goods and turned his attention to the new arrivals. Other than the rather seedy appearance of most, and especially, he thought, of one in a workman's cap pulled low around his ears, there was nothing very remarkable about them. He knew them to be the hooligan friends of the man, Wiggins, he'd seen earlier. Once, they were the scourge of every costermonger and shopkeeper in the area, only saved from certain and well-deserved confinement in a borstal by their friendship with Sherlock Holmes who called them his Baker Street Irregulars and involved them in highly suspect activities in the course of his own investigations. Now, older and supposedly wiser, they were believed to have turned respectable although obviously still not above taking the occasional run at a job for Mr. Holmes that undoubtedly would again put them close to the line. Indeed, he could see Wiggins, their one-time leader, heartily welcoming them to 221B, no doubt to describe to them their latest mission and await the arrival of Holmes. That would, however, be for others to sort, his only concern was with seeing the five who walked into the lodgings walk themselves back out.

Nearly an hour later he considered his job done. He'd seen five aging delinquents enter and now exit 221B. They commandeered two coaches whose drivers eyed them with the suspiciousness he felt they merited. He'd report it up the line, if only to show he was on the job, but he was certain his report would be filed and forgotten—or more likely filed unread with nothing therefore to forget. If he'd been trained by Mrs. Hudson, he would have seen that the man with the workman's cap pulled low had lost two full inches in the course of his time in the lodgings house. But he had not been trained by Mrs. Hudson and, in the words of someone who had, "He saw but did not observe." He missed taking note of the fact that while a scruffy Dr. Watson was beneath the workman's cap going into 221B, a scruffy Thomas Wiggins was beneath the workman's cap coming out.

The two carriages carrying their buxom female passengers arrived at the terraced home of Inspector Lestrade at times sufficiently well-spaced as to make an observer unaware there was any connection between the two. An elderly prelate, his shoulders hunched under the weight of his unflagging concern for others, waited patiently for the woman in the first carriage to disembark, then bid the driver wait as he gathered himself to mount the step into his conveyance. From his bay window, Lestrade watched with a wry smile the charade that was Sherlock Holmes in the disguise he believed necessary to allow him to go unrecognized to Victoria Station. As he had informed a skeptical Dr, Watson, if he was to be away for a while, he needed to make a quick trip to Sussex Downs to see that his bees were properly attended to. It had been the doctor's position that the bees were perfectly capable of caring for themselves, but both he and Lestrade recognized it was not a winnable argument and settled for Holmes's promise to return to 221B by nightfall, or at least not long after.

Christabel Parkhurst and Annie Kenney were each welcomed by Lestrade's daughter, Millicent, who had been hastily summoned to provide an acceptable female presence in the house, Lestrade having decided that it was one thing to maintain two lawbreakers in one's home, and quite another to maintain two young unmarried ladies in the home of a lone male. He felt certain he could explain away the first but that Mrs. Lestrade would be unforgiving of the second. On learning of his role in harboring the suffragette fugitives,

Millicent gave him a hug that would have rivaled Wiggins's earlier effort, kissed him on his cheek and, all in all, appeared more impressed with him that she had in a very long time—not, he thought, since he correctly guessed her wish for a bull terrier pup on her twelfth birthday.

In response to his mysterious request that she pack a large quantity of women's clothing "for women about your size," Millicent had brought a portmanteau stuffed with women's clothing volunteered by her and her roommates, the roommates' contribution coming with a promise to keep secret their donation in exchange for Millicent's promise of a detailed explanation of the use to which that clothing was put on her return. When all the introductions were complete and at least some of the situation clarified, Lestrade warned his guests that they shouldn't plan on staying longer than the week his wife would be away, but by then Millicent had started up the stairs to show them their bedchambers, and their curiosity about sleeping arrangements, and the treasures Millicent's portmanteau might hold, captured their full attention.

Chapter 3.
The Investigation Begins

With all members of the consulting detective agency reunited at 221B, the detectives were free to take up the investigation of Reginald Miles's death and, not incidentally, to absolve Watson of responsibility for that death. Watson made abundantly clear, if there could have been any doubt, his delight to be once again with his old friends and comrades in arms although he noted as well he would have wished for their meeting to be under less trying circumstances. He thought it likely that Lestrade was feeling well rid of him and that the trade for two rock-throwing suffragettes would be seen by the inspector as well made. In fact, when Lestrade, himself, thought about the exchange, he conjured up images of frying pans and fires and the short distance between them.

"It would seem we have to interview all those who attended Watson's dinner," suggested Holmes, looking to Watson but speaking to Mrs. Hudson.

What Holmes had not yet fully grasped was the extent to which he was now trusted to employ his own judgment in the course of an investigation. Mrs. Hudson would continue to take lead responsibility for planning the investigative strategy, but it was Mrs. Hudson's belief that, over their years together, he had become sufficiently proficient to be allowed broad responsibility, albeit within the parameters she set. She had not yet chosen to share that information with Holmes but was confident he would nonetheless act as if she had just as he had always done.

"I quite agree, Mr. 'Olmes. We might first make a list of all those who were at your dinner, Dr. Watson."

Watson nodded and this once spoke without consulting his accounts book, which he nonetheless set before him to be available if needed. "I was at the head of the dinner table and, as I said earlier, I'd given the Smythes the day out for the time of the party. The absence of servants meant, of course, that I had to bring the roast to the table. I did have help from Margaret's sister, Violet, as well as Alice, Reginald's daughter-in-law, in getting the rest of the dishes to the table and later clearing them. I must say everyone was good about passing plates and dishing up for each other when it was called for.

"In terms of the rest of our seating, I put Reginald— Reginald, Senior—opposite me at the foot of the table. On my right was Mrs. Eugenia Clark, then came her husband, Henry. In what must have been happier times, the Clarks had been near neighbors and friends of Reginald and his wife, Natalie. That, of course, was before Reginald and Natalie divorced. In any event, the Clarks turned out to be a pleasant if rather bland couple. Certainly not my cup of tea but if I had wanted to learn the secrets to growing prize-winning roses or hear, in excruciating detail, the intricacies of the apothecary trade, I was perfectly positioned.

"Fortunately for me, next down from the Clarks were the two younger Mileses—Edward, Reginald's only son, and Alice, his wife. As I've said, Edward is not the young man's given first name, which is, in fact, Reginald, Junior. As if refusing to use his father's name wasn't sufficient proof of the rift between father and son, Edward seemed intent on driving the point home all through dinner. In spite of his father being next to him at the foot of the table, both Edward and Alice directed the vast majority of their conversation toward me or others at the table. And to tell the truth, at the time that suited me just fine. Edward shared remembrances of Margaret that rang bittersweet under the circumstances but were of far greater interest to me than anything the Clarks had to offer. And it wasn't just me that was interested in the memories Edward shared. It seemed to me a good many hung on his words and several asked questions. Even Reginald, who must have known most, if not all of Edward's stories, remained attentive and occasionally elaborated briefly on some aspect of his son's stories." Watson paused to consider whether he had omitted anything significant, decided he had not, and continued around the dinner table.

"Reginald was seated next and, as I've said, was at the opposite end of the table from me. In the main, Reginald was content to let others carry the conversation except, as I say, for occasional comments elaborating on his son's contributions. Nor, I must say, were his opinions or ideas solicited. I'm afraid that, in spite of Margaret's hopes and plans, Reginald had so cut himself off from everyone at the table that I saw no real chance of reconciliation.

"I, of course, didn't get along with Reginald any much better than any of the others, very possibly worse than many of the others—since, as I said earlier, for whatever reason, he seemed intent on attacking me.

"You should understand that during Margaret's lifetime I tried to remain civil. To be fair, I think we both did. I'm sure Margaret knew we rubbed each other the wrong way and we simply agreed not to talk about it. In any event, after Margaret's death, and more particularly after the reading of Margaret's will, whatever civility he had practiced all but disappeared. He mumbled something to me about promises made, but I had no idea what he was talking about. He seemed to have expected some sort of endowment from Margaret to make up for his getting very little from their father's will. Whatever it was that rankled him, he was intent on making me his whipping boy for the evening.

"There's things you should know about my father-in-law's will, although he wasn't my father-in-law at the time. As a result of her inheritance Margaret was quite well to do. Her father had modified his will after Margaret's first husband, Arnold, died. Arnold had little to leave her as he was still building his business when he passed away. Her father was intent on leaving Margaret sufficiently free of concerns about finances to make certain she would never have to marry simply to stay solvent. In fact, his will was crafted so that even if she married, she would retain control of her own inheritance for her lifetime. It was, in truth, something we both wanted anyway and so it placed no burden on our marriage. We agreed to live on my income alone and that's what we did right up to the day she died.

"Margaret's sister, Violet, was married, and therefore seen as not being in need of similar protection. Her husband, Stanford, was in banking, in a junior position at the time, but he was seen as certain to advance which made for a smaller legacy for her. Unfortunately, the rise in status and income has never materialized, leaving the Johnsons quite frustrated I suspect. And, of course, their father provided even less for Reginald, whom he considered to be a wastrel. Her father died before we married, so there were no further changes to his will. Margaret's own will made me her sole heir, which, as I've said, seemed to come as an unpleasant surprise to Reginald.

Margaret always felt a little uncomfortable—really, more than a little—about her inheritance as compared to her sister's and brother's. Nonetheless, she thought what was right was to make me her sole heir so that, as her husband, I'd be taken care of in case of sudden unforeseen circumstances. But barring that, all of her inheritance would pass to her sister and brother when I was gone. Violet and Reginald knew about that arrangement, and, whatever their feelings, it was never discussed.

"I should make clear as well, I never had a problem with any of Margaret's family except for her brother—and I was far from alone there. I don't know how any of this relates to Reginald's death—if any of it relates at all—but I think it's well for you to know about my relationship with the family.

In any event, let me get back to enumerating the dinner guests. I left off with Reginald at the foot of the table. On his right, which is to say far down the table to my left, was Cyril Worthington, a onetime close friend of Reginald's—his closest from what he told me, although he also said they had drifted apart over the last several years.

He was, to my mind, a most welcome addition to the dinner party. He seemed the kind of person who is in perpetual good humor and determined to see to it that everyone around him shares his good feeling. Not even he could lighten the mood for long, but it might have been a good deal darker if not for his efforts. He knew Reginald and Margaret as children and seemed to have a score of anecdotes going back to that time. I must say, after hearing stories of their growing up together, I had a better sense of why Margaret, in spite of everything, continued to have good feelings for her brother.

"In any event, continuing around the table, next there was Violet and Stanford Johnson. Violet is, if I haven't said already, Margaret's older sister. She only agreed to attend the dinner because it promised to be a tribute to Margaret, but I was well aware she neither liked nor trusted Reginald.

"The final dinner guest, and the one on my immediate left, was Wilson James, Reginald's one time business partner. He said very little to anyone and nothing to Reginald as best as I could tell. Indeed, when we were alone, he asked me why he had been invited. When I told him it was because he and Reginald were in business together, he said that was the last reason he could think of for inviting him. I had no idea what he meant by that, and he moved away before I could ask."

"If ever a dinner party appeared headed for disaster, Watson, this was clearly it," Holmes shook his head in cheerless sympathy with his friend.

Watson fixed his face in a grimace, not in disagreement, but rather to acknowledge the fate he had felt himself powerless to avoid.

"Don't forget, Holmes, the get-together was virtually Margaret's dying wish." While Holmes groaned his understanding, Mrs. Hudson sought to take the conversation in a direction that would lead to a consideration of the action now to be taken.

"We can presume one or more of Dr. Watson's dinner guests is a murderer. You 'ave their addresses from the invitations, Doctor. We might just as well interview each of the guests in the order you presented them."

With one part of their investigative strategy delineated, Holmes spoke to a second aspect that had been troubling him throughout their discussion. "We know that Watson cannot accompany me in interviewing suspects, and that he has, in the past, frequently provided significant assistance on that score, especially in maintaining a record that helped guide the steps in our investigation." He gave Watson an indulgent smile and received Watson's blank stare. "How then shall we proceed with Watson no longer able to play that role?"

Lest someone suggest an option other than the one he had already chosen, Holmes answered his own question without allowing himself another breath. "I could, of course, ask all the questions we agree on and then record my findings immediately after the interview." Mrs. Hudson's curled lip and hard squint led Holmes to try an additional and somewhat desperate proposal. "There's also Wiggins. You know he's come a long way since his days as a page and he is knowledgeable about this case."

It was now Watson's turn to give Holmes a hard squint as he contemplated relying on a reformed petty thief to save him from the gallows. It was left to Mrs. Hudson to voice the proposal that was, in fact, more than just a proposal.

36

"I believe two sets of ears and two 'eads will be needed, Mr. 'Olmes, and I'm afraid Thomas is not the answer. 'E's been 'elpful in many ways, but 'e doesn't know 'ow we go about conductin' an investigation—and 'e could be more of a 'indrance than a 'elp if 'e was to start practicin' now. Besides which, 'e doesn't know anythin' about the way we run our consultin' detective agency and that's the way we want to keep it. No, it's got to be me that goes along with you, Mr. 'Olmes, and we need a reason for my bein' with you. We'll want somethin' that's simple, believable, and not goin' to lead to a whole lot of questions.

"I'm thinkin' we can say this is a special case that can benefit from gettin' a woman's point of view. Let it go at that and then move on to the questions we will have worked out before anybody 'as a chance to comment or raise a question about what's been said."

Mrs. Hudson then gave a vivid illustration of the behavior she was recommending. Without allowing opportunity for a comment or question, she moved the conversation to the area of concern to her. "I believe we should now get started workin' out the questions we'll want to ask the Clarks. We'll need two sets of questions. 'E will be at 'is apothecary shop and she will almost certainly be at 'ome. I'll put up a pot of tea and there are a few scones left from earlier. That will 'ave to 'old us for now." She looked questioningly to her colleagues. There was no dissent.

With preparation for the next day's questioning of Edith and Henry Clark complete, and questions for Alice and Edward Miles developed for good measure, a hearty dinner was consumed as the just reward for a hard day's work. After which, with a nod of appreciation to Mrs. Hudson, Holmes and Watson went upstairs to the sitting room to share a last pipe of the day while Mrs. Hudson went to her kitchen to attend to the dishes collected in her tub. As she scrubbed dishes that had earlier held vegetable soup, lamb stew, and bread pudding, the sudden reunion of the three members of London's foremost consulting detective agency stirred memories of its bittersweet beginnings.

Her colleagues would count its start with the advertisement she placed in the London newspapers reading "rooms to let, good location, applicants should possess an inquiring mind and curiosity about human behavior." The ad attracted the attention of a tall, slender chemist with a commanding air and precise Cambridge diction. The possessor of those traits seemed to her as perfect a figurehead for the organization she planned to establish as would be possible to find. That he brought with him the level-headed Dr. John Watson was a further and very strong point in his favor. A consulting detective agency was forged on the spot.

And still she knew better than to count that as the agency's beginning. That occurred long before; so long before that Mrs. Hudson could not recall the exact date although she would never forget the event itself. After dinner one night she suggested to Tobias that, to allow her to learn more about his work as a constable, they search the *Evening Standard* for the report of a suitable crime, for which he would describe the action likely to be taken by the police; then, together, they would describe the actions that could be taken as part of their own, more comprehensive, criminal investigation. It instantly became an every-evening event, only changing in two aspects. They soon dropped a consideration of police routine, instead focusing solely on the creation of their own investigative strategy, and, while initially Tobias always took the lead in that creation, over time, Mrs. Hudson took an ever larger role, until finally, she, not infrequently, took the lead with Tobias contributing encouragement rather than direction.

She called Tobias her "uncommon common constable" as they followed the pattern he had suggested.

They would first describe and analyze the crime scene. That would lead to a determination of the clues available, the additional information needed and a strategy for gathering that information, including, most particularly, decisions regarding the people needing to be interviewed and the questions needing to be put to them. Nor did her education rest solely on what she learned in her evening sessions with Tobias. There were also weekly trips to the library to borrow books dealing with poisons, guns, knives, drownings, and the effects of various blunt instruments. Library staff showed some initial alarm while fulfilling her requests. They were only partly reassured by her cheerful, if business-like demeanor, but were more largely reassured by the absence of any reports of grisly crimes committed by middle-aged ladies in the days following her visit.

Nor did she count her education complete even with the addition of the library's reference works. A good detective, she felt, had to have a capacity to read people. To that end, she made careful study of the people she saw on her visits to the greengrocer, the butcher, and the post office, as well as those she passed on the street or saw making purchases from costermongers. She studied how they carried themselves, their dress, their facial expressions, and the way they related to other people; then tested herself as to what she could conclude about the people she observed and with what degree of confidence she could draw those conclusions.

Mrs. Hudson smiled sadly at the memories stirred. She felt certain she would be alone in reminiscing about the beginnings of the consulting detective agency. In that, at least, she was wrong. The origins of 221B Baker Street were the subject of discussion upstairs as well. To be sure, Holmes and Watson had no memory of most of the things Mrs. Hudson remembered, and remembered other things differently than Mrs. Hudson, but they remembered all things with the same sad smile.

At eleven o'clock Mrs. Hudson and a less than enthusiastic Holmes entered the semicircular carriage path that led past a carefully tended flower garden to the front porch of the Clarks's three-story home. The house, with its richly windowed turret on one side, huge bay window on the other, and the promise of spacious living quarters within, spoke eloquently of the material success the Clarks had made of their lives.

After asking their coachman to wait, they climbed the steps to the covered porch and rang the bell to summon Mrs. Clark, or more likely, they thought, the Clarks's housekeeper. In fact, they got both in rapid succession. Upon hearing Holmes introduce himself and Mrs. Hudson, Mrs. Clark emerged from where she was standing unseen behind the open door, relieving the housekeeper of any further responsibility for her visitors.

Mrs. Clark was of a height that made both Mrs. Hudson and Holmes acutely aware of a need to straighten where they stood. Holmes was not, in fact, challenged by the woman's height, but Mrs. Hudson was certain a good number of men and most women would be. Mrs. Clark, herself, appeared oblivious to the impression she made, going so far as to dress in a manner that accentuated her still slender figure thereby accentuating her height as well.

She stepped back, allowing admittance as far as the entry hall but not yet beyond. "Good morning, Mr. Holmes, ma'am, I am Mrs. Eugenia Clark." Having given the obligatory greeting to Mrs. Hudson, whose presence was a mystery to her, she turned her full attention to the man she knew if only by reputation. "Mr. Holmes, as I tried to make clear on the telephone to your assistant, whoever she was, out of respect for you and your work, I have agreed to meet with you although I cannot imagine how I can be of any help to you in your investigation … if that's what this is." Eugenia

Clark waited a moment to allow a response from Holmes. Receiving none, she salvaged what she could in appearing to control the events unfolding in her own home. I will try to oblige you in what time I can make available. We can meet in my parlor." As she turned to lead the way, she seemed to recall that the situation called for some minimal hostess duties. "I'll ask cook to bring tea and some of her excellent scones."

"The scones sound a special treat," said Holmes. Mrs. Hudson said nothing.

Mrs. Clark's parlor appeared to Mrs. Hudson to reflect the personality of its mistress. Both seemed to exhibit elegance without warmth. Entering the room, the eye traveled first to the far wall, where a pianoforte stood beside a window whose velvet curtains were tied back by pale rose sashes. Mrs. Hudson noted that no music books were visible and wondered about the instrument's use. In another corner a generously damasked round table supported a large urn on which dozens of small blue flowers were painted in helter-skelter fashion, the blue of the flowers a match for the blue of the damask cover. A chaise lounge was to their immediate left, while three armed easy chairs and a single unarmed chair were set around a low table in support of conversation between herself and invitees to her home. After giving her guests a moment to admire the room, Mrs. Clark waved a hand in the general direction of the table leaving it to Holmes and Mrs. Hudson to make selections from the armed easy chairs while she occupied the unarmed chair.

Settling herself in one of the armed easy chairs, Mrs. Hudson set about studying their reluctant hostess. She had regular features, excepting for a somewhat weak chin while streaks of gray were beginning to invade auburn hair. Indeed, Mrs. Hudson was surprised to find herself viewing the woman as rather good-looking. Only her temperament was against her. She made no secret of resenting this intrusion into her day. Mrs. Hudson was certain it reflected her way of relating to the world that was at once sour and imperious.

"What is it you believe I can tell you about the death of Reginald Miles? It's my understanding, Mr. Holmes, that this Dr. Watson is a long-time friend and so you may have a particular interest in looking into his charge." With that she settled back in her chair and awaited the inquiry she had deemed to be both pointless and biased.

Before Holmes could respond, the woman, who had answered the bell on his and Mrs. Hudson's arrival, entered the room with a trayful of refreshments. Without looking to any of the people she served, she poured three cups of tea and set milk, sugar and lemon in the center of the low table together with three small plates and a platter holding six scones, afterward departing with only a softly spoken, "ma'am," still without having made eye contact with anyone.

Holmes ignored the woman's characterization of his interest in the murder of Reginald Miles, instead choosing only to affirm his belief in the necessity of further investigation, while Mrs. Hudson selected a scone for the purpose of making an inquiry of her own.

"I recognize the police believe they have correctly identified the person who killed Reginald Miles. I have reason to believe otherwise and am concerned that the person punished for the crime is the person who perpetrated the crime. As you may know, I have successfully carried out many similar investigations. Based on those experiences, I believe it imperative that we interview the people who were at Dr. Watson's dinner party the night Reginald Miles was killed and that we hear the recollections of everyone who was a witness to the events of that evening."

Eugenia Clark nodded reluctant understanding of Holmes's explanation and intent, before raising a question about one aspect of his investigation. "As I say, I've read of

Mr. Holmes. I don't believe I've ever seen mention of a ... Mrs. Hudson, is it?"

For the moment, Mrs. Hudson held at bay the scone she had chosen. With a small smile she responded to Mrs. Clark in accord with her earlier advice for dealing with such comments. "It is Mrs. 'Udson, and I am 'ere because Mr. 'Olmes believes there's things about the case that can benefit from gettin' a woman's point of view."

Eugenia Clark said nothing, but her eyebrows crept just a tiny bit closer to her forehead. The statement made perfect sense but appeared out of synch with the person who spoke it. In any event, there appeared to be nothing to do other than to answer their questions as briefly as possible to get rid of them as quickly as possible. "What is it you want to know?" she asked, now addressing both of her visitors.

As had been agreed, Holmes took the lead. "I'm hoping you can reconstruct events of the evening's dinner party as you remember them. I believe you were seated to Dr. Watson's right and Mr. Clark was to your right."

"That's correct."

"How would you characterize the conversation at the dinner table? Did you have any sense of the tragedy that was to follow?"

Mrs. Clark pursed her lips before responding to Holmes. "Certainly not from the conversation at our end of the table. Which was, in fact, quite friendly. Your Dr. Watson was a most engaging dinner companion and, I have to say, seemed to be in rather good spirits for someone about to commit a murder—although of course I've no idea how someone about to commit a murder might appear."

"And at the other end of the table?"

"I didn't concern myself with what was happening at the other end of the table. I mostly tried not to look in that direction. Still, early on and for a while, everything seemed to be peaceful there as well. In fact, if I didn't know any better, I'd say we were all getting along just fine. But of course, I did know better. Everyone at the table knew better, as I'm sure do you. There was long-standing tension between Reginald and his son. As one part of that, it looked to me as if Edward directed his conversation almost entirely toward us or across the table to his aunt and uncle and avoided his father. Indeed, I would guess that helped keep things as peaceful as they were early on." Having shared as much as she cared to, Mrs. Clark paused to bite into the end of the scone she'd taken from the tray and warily awaited further questioning.

"Why do you say 'early on', Mrs. Clark? Did things change over the course of the evenin'?"

She delayed her response long enough to take a second bite of her scone before speaking. "I think all who were there would agree things changed. I suppose it was the combination of the wine and the feelings people were trying to hold back. And that included Reginald, who seemed to be terribly upset with Dr. Watson. Anyway, that was when somebody suggested we wait a bit before taking dessert and look at the photographs Dr. Watson had taken of his and Margaret's trip to the Highlands. That did seem to settle things down, but then, when we got back to the table, the tragedy occurred. We drank a toast to Margaret and, within what seemed like seconds, Reginald fell dead across the table. But not before pointing to Dr. Watson and accusing him of murder. I'm sorry but we all saw it, Mr. Holmes."

Her story told, Mrs. Clark refreshed herself with several small sips of the tea poured for her earlier. Mrs. Hudson took the moment to take an experimental bite of the scone she'd chosen. In spite of herself, she breathed a small sigh of relief as she set the remainder of the scone back on her plate, before turning her attention to what she saw as the untold portion of Mrs. Clark's story.

"I'm wonderin', Mrs. Clark, about the time spent lookin' at Dr. Watsons's photographs. Did people stay in the study the whole time before goin' back to the dining room or did people move around durin' that time?"

"I'd have to say there was a great deal of traffic in and out of the study—or I suppose it would be more accurate to say out and then back into the study. It wouldn't surprise me to learn that everyone left the study at one time or another. I did myself and so did Mr. Clark. To tell you the truth, I was quite curious to see what changes your Dr. Watson had made to Margaret's home since I last saw it. Violet Johnson, Margaret's sister, was equally curious and, as we had agreed, she left the study the same time Mr. Clark and I did. The two of us, that is to say, Violet and I, made a kind of tour of the house as I'm sure she'll tell you. In fact, we were both pleased to see there had been very few changes made. And if you have it in mind to ask about Mr. Clark's whereabouts, I can't say for sure, but I believe he went to have a smoke by himself since he knows I abhor the smell of cigarettes."

Correctly presuming the next question from Mrs. Hudson, Mrs. Clark continued to describe her memory of the evening of Reginald Miles's death. "And please don't ask me for specifics in terms of who left the study when, and when they came back. If I try to do that, I will undoubtedly leave someone out and perhaps incorrectly report someone who stayed as having gone out. I'll not have that on my conscience so I will not give you any names." To make her position clear, she clamped her mouth shut and jutted her jaw toward her interrogator. It seemed clear to that interrogator that a change of subject was in order.

"You say, Mrs. Clark, you tried not to look to the other end of the table. I couldn't 'elp wonderin' why that would be? Was there somethin' or maybe somebody you wanted to avoid?" Mrs. Hudson smiled as if her question expressed nothing more than idle curiosity.

It gave every sign of awakening more than idle curiosity in Mrs. Clark. Having successfully terminated one line of questioning, she thought she might achieve the same objective with another.

"I'm afraid that gets into a rather private area, Mrs. Hudson, that I have no wish to explore. I assure you it has nothing to do with Reginald's poisoning."

"I quite appreciate your feelings, Mrs. Clark," Holmes contorted his face to what he hoped was a show of that appreciation, "but there has been a murder and I must insist you be appropriately forthcoming and allow us to judge what is or is not relevant to our investigation. I assure you both Mrs. Hudson and I will treat whatever you tell us with the utmost discretion."

Mrs. Clark wavered, then set her jaw in continuing obstinance. "I can't see how anything I would say in that area could be relevant to your investigation. Indeed, I believe it will only lead to wholly unnecessary and unpleasant discussion."

A gentler but equally firm voice made clear the need for the woman's report as well as suggesting a strategy for getting past the issues that she thought might explain Mrs. Clark's reticence. "It's the case, I'm afraid, where nothin' that involves Mr. Reginald Miles or Dr. Watson can be counted as not 'avin' relevance. But we've no wish to do anythin' that would lead to unnecessary difficulty. I wonder, would it make sense for us to discuss things woman to woman, rememberin' that, like Mr. 'Olmes says, we've no interest in tittle-tattle."

Again, Mrs. Clark wavered, again she set her jaw, but this time she let it relax after fortifying herself with a last swallow of the tea still in her cup. "I take it you are a married woman, Mrs. Hudson."

"I was for twenty-nine years. I'm a widow now."

"And you are a life-long bachelor, Mr. Holmes."

46

Holmes gave a long nod.

"It might be well for us married folk to have a talk while you take a turn around the gardens in back, Mr. Holmes. You'll find several varieties of roses, many of which have won prizes. I'm quite proud of our gardens."

With Holmes dispatched and a fresh pot of tea set down by the nameless housekeeper, Mrs. Clark began a description of people and events that Mrs. Hudson saw as very possibly tied to Reginald Miles's death in spite of Mrs. Clark's earlier protest. She noted, as well, that although Mrs. Clark experienced some initial difficulty in its telling, in time it seemed to become nearly a comfort to air her story to someone who seemed capable of understanding her dilemma, and not unimportantly Mrs. Hudson thought, someone she expected never to see again. The story turned out, however, to be unexpectedly discomfiting for her understanding listener.

"Let me say first, Mrs. Hudson, I hold my husband in the highest regard."

Mrs. Hudson nodded soberly as she knew was expected of her.

"He's a good man and an excellent provider."

There was a second nod, deeper than the first.

Her recognition of her husband's positive features established, she took a deep breath and began to describe events she had hoped never to have to explore. "You're a married woman or, anyway you have been, and you know the needs of a woman and the expectations in a marriage. And you know it happens sometimes that a man busies himself and commits all of his energy to making something of himself in the world, which is to say in his world, while a woman wants a show of affection from her husband more often than maybe he's wanting to give it. I don't know if you've had the experience, Mrs. Hudson, but I don't believe it's all that unusual." She waited hopefully, but doubtfully for

Mrs. Hudson's response. After several seconds Mrs. Hudson met her doubts but not her hopes.

"Of course, I know what you're sayin' but I can't say it's somethin' I experienced myself. I was just that fortunate to 'ave the best of men for too short a time."

Eugenia Clark nodded her unsurprise.

"I am happy for your good fortune, Mrs. Hudson, and sorry it was cut short." Mrs. Hudson nodded her appreciation of the woman's words.

"I want it to be clear from the beginning, the fault for my situation was mine alone—at least at first. In the early days, in the happier days, we were near neighbors living several houses apart on the same street with Reginald and Natalie, his wife at the time. We had dinners at each other's house, played whist together and, on at least a couple of occasions went to concerts together. We became close friends as both Mr. Clark and I saw it at the time. There were instances when Reginald would stop by alone during the day, sometimes on behalf of Natalie to plan for the dinner we'd be having together, or to bring by things I might need if we were having dinner at our house. We were never alone, however. There was always the butler or housekeeper, usually both. Mr. Clark would, of course, be at his shop all day. Reginald, on the other hand, was involved in buying and selling properties and could keep his own hours. Anyway, as I say, there was always one or both of the servants in the house when he came to visit, until one day there wasn't." Mrs. Clark raised her teacup from its saucer, deliberated for a moment, then set the cup firmly back down.

"I could say he took advantage of me, but it wouldn't be quite true. As I've suggested, Mr. Clark was intent on creating a successful business to support the two of us and, beyond that, to provide some of the luxuries we'd talked about being able to afford someday. If Reginald didn't take advantage of me, he certainly took advantage of the situation.

I can only say, Mrs. Hudson, I was appalled by what I'd done and swore on the spot never to allow anything like that to happen again. And I've kept my promise, Mrs. Hudson, although Reginald tried many times to get me to break it. But that's not all of it or maybe even the worst of it." This time the teacup made it all the way to her lips. After a long swallow, she was ready to share the worst.

"It's three … more than three years since that time. Natalie divorced herself from Reginald when she learned for herself the kind of man he was and went to live with her family in York until her death nearly a year ago. Reginald moved away as well, but that didn't end things between us— not by a long shot. He kept after me. At first, he kept trying to get me to repeat my mistake. When it was clear I wouldn't do that, he demanded I meet him at some out of the way place, and that I bring some designated amount of money that he needed to borrow from me. It was never a great deal, nothing I couldn't get from the household accounts, but I was always given to understand that if I didn't get it for him, he would inform Mr. Clark of my indiscretion—and in his own colorful language, I'm sure. For a while at least, the payments seemed endless. More recently, they seemed to stop and, in fact, I hadn't heard from Reginald for a good many months. Now that I know I'll never hear from him again, I hope to blot him permanently from my memory.

"I can tell you, Mrs. Hudson, I feel no sadness about Reginald's death. I freely admit I feel quite the contrary and am grateful to Dr. Watson for ridding him from my world."

With that said, Mrs. Hudson took temporary refuge in her teacup as she considered how to respond to a narrative for which neither yesterday's practice session nor her life had prepared her. Having drawn whatever counsel was available from her teacup, she attempted to fill the silence that followed Mrs. Clark's confession.

"I am truly sorry. You've 'ad to endure more than any woman ever should. I'd say you're a wonderful, strong woman to be doin' as well as you are."

Mrs. Clark soberly nodded her appreciation for Mrs. Hudson's comment. "One simply does what one must. You can see why I was reluctant to share this with you."

"Of course, and I will not be sharin' it beyond Mr. 'Olmes who, I can tell you, is totally trustworthy. I've known 'im these good many years and 'ave never known 'im to break a trust." Mrs. Hudson paused before describing what the woman's story suggested to her as a prudent, if difficult, course of action. "I can't 'elp but wonder if it wouldn't be the right time to let Mr. Clark know the terrible problems you've 'ad to deal with. With Reginald Miles no longer in your life, you don't 'ave to worry about what 'e could say and you can describe things the way you think they should be described. It just strikes me as bein' an awful secret to 'ave to carry through a marriage."

What Mrs. Hudson didn't say was that, regardless of hers and Mr. Holmes's efforts, the woman's story could well come to light in the course of a police investigation. Then, she would have the unhappy task of convincing the authorities of her innocence in the death of the man who had been blackmailing her and could resume doing so at any time, a man conveniently seated next to her at dinner. And when that was done, she would have the challenge of explaining away her actions to Mr. Clark. Her suggestion made, Mrs. Hudson again retreated into her teacup.

"It's been a burden to carry, I don't deny that, Mrs. Hudson, but I'll need to think about what you say. You know how men can react to such news." Mrs. Hudson nodded her affirmation of information she did not possess.

They rejoined Holmes only briefly before deciding they had best get on with their day. Whatever that might have meant for Mrs. Clark, for Holmes and Mrs. Hudson, it meant a trip to an apothecary.

Mrs. Hudson's report of her conversation with Mrs. Clark took up the whole of their carriage ride to see Mr. Clark except for Holmes's occasional questions largely designed to deepen Mrs. Hudson's blush. Nonetheless, when they reached the apothecary, both of them shared a concern with knowing whether Mr. Clark was aware of his wife's history and, if he was, whether that awareness could have led to murder.

Mr. Clark dropped his welcoming smile on learning the names and purpose of the two visitors he had mistaken for customers. Stopping only to inform his shop assistant that he could be called if needed, he motioned for Holmes and Mrs. Hudson to join him as he disappeared behind the curtain that kept the intricacies of his art hidden from public view. There was only a single stool in the apothecary's work area, which all three ignored for the time of the interview.

Henry Clark was a balding man with the slight paunch that helped affirm his success in the world. Both Mrs. Hudson and Holmes had been curious to see how tall Mr. Clark would be. As he now stood before them, they each concluded he would be somewhat, but not a great deal taller than his wife. Like Mrs. Clark, he attempted to take control of the situation in hopes of bringing the exchange to a quick end.

"Of course, I want to be helpful in any way I can, but it was my understanding the police had concluded their investigation and were satisfied they had the offender in custody."

Holmes again described what he believed to be the rush to judgment by the police, contrasting their action with his own deliberate examination of the situation, then added a comment he thought might hasten the apothecary's cooperation.

"I should tell you that we spoke with Mrs. Clark earlier this morning and she was quite helpful." Clark nodded his awareness of information he already had, having spoken on the telephone with Mrs. Clark a short time before.

"Can you tell me … us something of your relationship with the murder victim?"

Before speaking, the apothecary carefully moved a beaker a greater distance from the edge of the counter although it appeared in no danger of falling. "It varied over time. I suppose my wife has told you the Mileses once lived within a few houses of us. We had some interests in common and socialized from time to time. That was, of course, before he and Natalie started having difficulties and eventually divorced. Those situations are always tricky when you see yourself as friends of both parties. You can't very well take sides, so, like it or not, you end up as we did—not seeing either of them. In any event, it wasn't long before each of them moved away and the problem, such as it was, was solved for us. Truthfully, Mr. Holmes, it feels like a hundred years ago and there's been a good deal of water under the bridge since then." He looked quizzically to Holmes waiting to hear of a connection between past and present and was not disappointed.

"The man you elected to stop seeing was murdered, poisoned in fact, at a dinner party you attended. As an investigator, I would be remiss if I did not question each guest who was present at his poisoning, perhaps especially a guest who is an apothecary."

"I trust you don't have it in mind to make an accusation, Mr. Holmes. Indeed, I would like to know under whose authority you are conducting your investigation. I know the police have already determined that Dr. John Watson murdered Mr. Miles, and it is well known that this

Watson is a friend of yours. Is that the basis for your interest in this case?"

Clark's voice had risen to a level unlikely to be contained by the flimsy curtain. It was then that a soft, calming voice intervened, albeit in a somewhat offputting dialect.

"I'm sure you're aware, Mr. Clark, that Mr. 'Olmes is often called in by Scotland Yard when they 'ave need of 'is skills to confirm their thinkin' or to take a different line as a kind of check on their thinkin'. Of course, they can't always let anyone know they're doin' that." She gave a long confidential nod to Clark that Holmes would later describe to Watson as containing a wink, which was then vehemently denied by Mrs. Hudson.

Henry Clark looked hard at Mrs. Hudson uncertain what to make of this middle-aged woman who spoke as if she might have been Holmes's scullery maid. It was not just her comment which, in any event, he didn't find wholly convincing. It was hearing it in a Cockney accent from a woman whose very presence was a mystery to him. It now seemed to him as it had to Mrs. Clark that his best course was to answer these people's questions as quickly and as briefly as possible and get back to a world free of inconvenient surprises.

"What then do you want to know from me?"

As it turned out, Clark had little to add to the account of the evening his wife had given a short time before. He spoke with arms folded tight across his chest and brows knit, unhappy at being questioned and seeing no reason to hide his unhappiness. He, too, described an affable Watson, an effort by all to be on good behavior, and, when that showed signs of failing, a brief respite in Watson's study to admire his photographs. Like his wife, he recalled a great deal of movement from the study and back to it, and, again like his wife, he was reticent to give names to those leaving and those staying lest he cast suspicion on someone erroneously or neglect to name someone he should have. The similarity in the accounts of the two Clarks gave further proof of their earlier collaboration.

He revealed he had been the first one to Reginald's side when he fell across the table, explaining that Dr. Watson had wanted to attend to Reginald, but it was deemed inappropriate for him to do so in light of Reginald's accusation. In the course of his description of events following the poisoning, the questions put to Clark moved him from reluctant witness to expert witness. In association with that change in status, his arms dropped to his sides and his forehead cleared of wrinkles.

"It was, in fact, an easy determination. Cyanide. The familiar smell of burnt almonds. You don't always get it— although most people think you do—but it was clearly there with Reginald. Of course, I said nothing about it to the others. It was a police matter so I only shared that kind of detail with the authorities.

Clark shared an empty smile with Holmes and Mrs. Hudson, convinced he had weathered the ordeal. Mrs. Hudson, however, wasn't quite done. Mr. Clark, like his wife, had the means and likely the opportunity to poison Reginald Miles. She suspected he had the motive as well. It remained for further questioning to corroborate that.

"I'm wonderin', Mr. Clark, we know so little about Mr. Miles. You knew 'im for a number of years. You and your wife did, I'm wonderin' what you can tell us about 'im."

The tell-tale arms were again clutched across his chest and his forehead furrowed as before. "I'm not much for judging personality. I leave that kind of thing to others. And besides, when Mrs. Clark and I knew Reginald, we knew him and Natalie as a couple and I … we looked at them that way. As I've said, when their marriage ended, we drifted apart. Ultimately, they left the area and that was the end of it. And now, I really should be getting back to my shop. We're near to the busy time of day and there are things I have to do to prepare." His visitors made no move to leave, and Clark steeled himself for another query.

"There's one more thing that bears checkin'. We've been told that Mr. Miles was quite the ladies' man. We're not yet sure 'ow that might figure into things, but it's an area we 'ave got to explore. Did you see any sign of that or maybe 'ear about it from someone?"

Holmes and Mrs. Hudson watched Clark's face as he heard the question and were rewarded with a sudden, if brief, pursing of his lips and rapid blinking of his eyes occurring in concert with the unconvincing denial he gave. "I wouldn't know anything about that. I'm sorry, I believe I've given you as much time as I have available. I have a business to run after all." This time Clark walked to the curtain and opened it wide as he urged his visitors to the door beyond and the ability to take back control of his life.

"I trust you have everything you need and there is no reason for our seeing each other again." He got an unsatisfying noncommittal grunt from Holmes and an indecipherable smile from Mrs. Hudson, who was now certain Mr. Clark had motive as well as means and opportunity.

Holmes and Mrs. Hudson made a brief stop at 221B, Holmes taking the opportunity to have a short talk with their shadow across the roadway. He brought with him two scones he intended as a parting gift and a request that he inform his superiors of the futility of his mission. The spy accepted the scones without a word of thanks or comment as to his future plans.

At Holmes's request, Mrs. Hudson made time for a quick and largely unsatisfactory lunch of buttered bread, a bit of leftover mutton and tea while they briefed Watson about the Clarks. It was then time to be off to interview Reginald Miles's son, Edward, and his wife, Alice.

Like the Lestrades, the Miles lived in a terraced housing development. There, however, the similarity ended. The Miles's home had no garden, no recessed entrance, and no bay window. It had only two tall windows on each of the home's two landings and all four windows lacked shutters. It did have one eye-catching feature. Within the housing's brick exterior, no two adjoining bricks seemed to have been fired to exactly the same color, although all were some shade of red or hinted at red. Some were flame red, some a more subdued russet, a few nearly orange. All of it made for a vivid impression on first-time visitors to the Miles's home, as it did now on Holmes and Mrs. Hudson.

Having gotten little information beyond a wish to meet regarding the death of Reginald Miles, Edward and Alice Miles greeted their visitors with as much warmth as two cautious people could muster. They managed wary smiles as they led their visitors to the flat's living room. The furniture they found there looked as if it might have been put together for them by a friend—and not a close friend. Edward and Alice Miles chose the room's sofa, while Mrs. Hudson chose the easy chair that held an almost plump cushion and Holmes made do with the remaining chair and its cushion's feeble attempt to provide comfort. It occurred to Mrs. Hudson that if the Mileses had planned in advance to make certain of a short visit, they couldn't have done any better than what was accomplished by happenstance.

A table to their left as they entered the room was nearly covered with stacks of paper, revealing it to be the Miles's version of a desk and filing cabinet combination. Atop a small mound of catalogues, Mrs. Hudson spied one from the Austrian furniture manufacturer, Thonet, a maker of bentwood chairs and other high-end furniture she had once briefly considered. There was no other table in the room making a non-issue of the non-offer of tea or other refreshment.

"I understand you have question about whether Dr. Watson killed my father. I thought the police were certain they had identified the right man." Edward Miles looked quizzically from Holmes to Mrs. Hudson and back to Holmes, his words and look reflecting confusion rather than dispute.

Holmes's soft-spoken response made clear his awareness of that distinction. "We feel your father's death demands a fuller investigation regardless of what's already been done.

"You'll have to forgive us, Mr. Holmes, ma'am, we were given the impression—in truth, we were told—that the police were confident they had identified my father-in-law's murderer," Alice Miles volunteered. "Of course, if there's any question, Edward and I want to help in any way we can." Edward Miles nodded vigorously in support of his wife's pledge of cooperation. Seizing on that pledge, Holmes and Mrs. Hudson began their questioning with the now familiar request that the respondents give their views of events the evening Reginald Miles died.

The account the two Miles provided was little more than a barebones reporting of the evening, adding little to what Holmes and Mrs. Hudson already knew, and thereby raising curiosity about what the Mileses might be holding back. On that account Mrs. Hudson decided to raise a more direct question. "You were sittin' closest to your father of anyone at the dinner table. 'Ow did things go between the two of you? What did you talk about?"

Miles shifted position where he sat before answering Mrs. Hudson. "The truth is we didn't talk. I was more interested in hearing what my uncle, Dr. Watson, had to say and I paid a lot more attention to that end of the table than the end where my father was."

"We already know, Mr. Miles, that you and your father didn't get along. Surely, that would also be reason for your not talkin' to each other."

Edward Miles shrugged. "Of course, there's no denying that, Mrs. Hudson. Still and all, your Dr. Watson is a most interesting man. And it wasn't just me who had read his stories and wanted to know more about his work with you, Mr. Holmes. And as for my father, while the way I came to deal with him was not to deal with him, there was nothing more to it. He's still my father and I could never do anything to hurt him no matter how I felt. Keeping my distance is one thing. Doing something ... like what happened is something else."

"And that's the God's honest truth, Mr. Holmes," Alice Miles looked to each as she spoke fervently in her husband's defense. "I know a wife is expected to support her husband, but this goes beyond just that. Edward simply couldn't do anything like what you're thinking. He doesn't even like to kill insects that get into our flat. If he has his way, he'll try to catch them and put them back outside."

Edward looked sheepishly to the hands in his lap but didn't deny his protection of the flat's insect population. Instead, he spoke to a suddenly awakened memory of the evening in question. "There's something else I should say about the dinner that night, or about my father at the dinner. To be fair, my father was mostly quiet nearly all through the meal. And it seemed like everybody was on good behavior through most of dinner. But there got to be a point where people started in on my father, joking at first, but then it got to be more than just joking. And my father got into it too. Except he wasn't joking. Mostly, he said things under his breath, but they were still loud enough to be heard by most everyone. And what he was saying was all about Uncle John

... Dr. Watson, nasty things like his sister shouldn't have married him, and how he was just after her money. Stuff like that. It had to be awful for Uncle John. I didn't know there was such bad feeling between them. That's when I suggested we take a break before dessert, and we look at the photographs Alice and I had already seen of Uncle John's and Aunt Margaret's trip to the Scottish Highlands.

"I guess I should explain about me and my father and how things got the way they did between us. Of course, early on, I was seeing him through a child's eyes and made allowances for his disappearing for periods and missing birthdays and things at school that other kids' fathers came to. When I got older, it was my Aunt Violet who got me to see him for what he was—a man without control of his gambling habit, which was why he'd be away until he ran out of money, except for some times when he'd had a lucky streak. Then, we might do one or maybe even two of the things he was always promising. Of course, Aunt Violet didn't tell me everything I found out later. Like about his using up money my mum needed to take care of me and the house, or about his borrowing. My mum never talked about it. She would tell me his work took him away for long periods and we just had to make do. As I got older, I came to see her frustration and realized she only stayed because of me, and when I was old enough to be on my own, she told me more about how she felt and explained why she had to leave our home. She invited me to go with her, but I was already seeing Alice and had a life here. She died before I ever got to see her again." Edward bit down on his lower lip, his eyes watering and threatening to overflow. Alice linked her arm through his and took his hand. It seemed to give Edward the strength to finish the history he'd begun. "It was only Aunt Margaret who kept believing he would see the light and change. I'm sure she believed it right up to the end. All the time it was Aunt Violet who got it right."

"You sound to be very close to your Aunt Violet." Mrs. Hudson sounded her most sympathetic.

Edward huffed his response. "I am. I don't see anything wrong with that." He looked from one to the other of his inquisitors making no effort to hide his disdain for them both.

"Is this the kind of thing you want to know. I can't see that it gets you anyplace but is it what you want?"

"It's useful in giving us the whole picture. You'd be amazed how even the smallest detail can have a major impact." Mrs. Hudson nodded approval of Holmes's unexpected comment, but he took no notice as he forged ahead with the questions they had worked out together.

'It's my understanding that not everyone remained in the study the whole time Dr Watson was showing his photographs. What do you remember about people leaving the study during that time?"

"What I remember is people going in and out the whole time my uncle was trying to tell about his and Aunt Margaret's trip. It seemed to me to be pretty much everybody, even Uncle John had to leave at one point to check on things in the kitchen, and I saw my father leave as well. Of course, not at the same time. Anyway, it didn't seem to me polite with everybody going in and out, besides which, I didn't like the way my father was going after Uncle John. With all that, Alice and I thought it was the right thing to stay in the study to show our support for Uncle John."

"And I'm sure it was appreciated," Holmes commented although Watson had said nothing about it. Mrs. Hudson supported Holmes to the extent of a half smile and nod, although she too had heard nothing from Watson about his nephew's action. After a pause that seemed to Holmes suitable, he raised question in another area of concern.

"I wonder if you know the terms of your Aunt Margaret's will, Mr. Miles?"

"I do. Yes. It was discussed after she died."

"Then you know your grandfather's fortune, which was largely willed to her, was to pass first to Dr. Watson, then to her brother and sister—your father and aunt. Do you know the contents of your father's will?"

Edward Miles slowly shook his head. "I don't. He never said and he certainly never invited questioning. Frankly, we've been going our separate ways for a very long time. I wouldn't expect him to suddenly change and give me any gift. Maybe he arranged to pay off the loan sharks and everybody else he owes. Who knows? Alice and I intend to just go on with our lives as we always have without thinking about an inheritance that's not likely to be there."

At the mention of her name, Alice Miles spoke to her own concern, "I suppose it's unavoidable that people will think we could benefit from this terrible thing through an inheritance, and I can't deny the money would come as a wonderful surprise. How can we avoid looking guilty of a terrible crime we'd never have anything to do with?"

It sounded less a question than a plea for help and Holmes spoke to that plea.

"You must respond with honesty and cooperation both with us and with the police when they come calling. Anything less than your full cooperation makes it appear you have something to hide. Mrs. Hudson and I will be continuing our investigation, and I fully expect we will know the truth regarding your father's death in a very few days. In the meantime, if you believe yourself innocent of any crime, you should act as though you are and get on with your lives as Edward suggests."

Holmes was by now anxious to vacate his less than comfortable chair and, turning to Mrs. Hudson, he asked hopefully, "I believe we've learned all we can, do you agree, Mrs. Hudson?"

Holmes got a small nod from Mr. Hudson, and the two of them rose to their feet. "I thank you both for giving us this time. If any additional questions come up, I trust we can count on you to be available." Both of the Miles gave less than enthusiastic nods of agreement as they led their visitors to the front door and back onto the London street.

On their return to Baker Street, Holmes looked first and with satisfaction to the empty place across the roadway. He was about to share his observation with Mrs. Hudson when she pointed out her own discovery. Their neighborhood patrolman, Constable Chase, was coming toward them from half a street away, displaying uncharacteristic speed. They waited first for him to catch up to them and then for him to catch his breath. When he was sufficiently recovered, the news he had to share seemed at first to do no more than confirm their own observations. Their watchdog from earlier times had been reassigned. The second part of what he had to share was new and welcome information. The constable's superiors wanted Mr. Holmes to know this signaled no relaxation in their surveillance or of their intent to take Dr. Watson into custody and that Constable Chase would be tracking the goings-on at 221B in the course of making his rounds. His warning of dire consequences if Dr. Watson was found there was undone by the wink he gave them coupled with the broad smile that quickly replaced the scowl he had briefly attempted.

"Frankly, Mr. Holmes, there's not a man in the station who don't think it's a put-up job and Dr. Watson is no more guilty of murdering someone than the man in the moon."

"Thank you, Constable, should I ever happen to see Dr. Watson, I'll let him know of the support he has."

Taking their leave from the constable, and smiling their satisfaction with the news, Holmes and Mrs. Hudson joined the object of the now relaxed vigil to apprise him of his changed status and of their visit to Edward and Alice Miles. As it turned out, Watson had his own news to share. He informed his colleagues that the phone had rung several times in the past hour. He had, of course, not answered, but he was certain that, given the frequency of calls, whoever it was would call again and likely quite soon.

As if to make a prophet of Watson, the phone rang minutes later as Mrs. Hudson and Holmes were nearing the end of briefing Watson on their day. With a knowing look to her colleagues, she went to take the call.

"'Ello," she hollered into the receiver. She did not yet wholly trust the new contraption, by itself, to cover the distance between herself and her caller. "Yes, this is Mrs. 'Udson. Good evenin', Inspector." With the pocket door open between the kitchen and the dinner table, she was guaranteed a respectfully alert audience for the length of the call.

At first, there was nothing to hear. What they could see was a lengthy period of Mrs. Hudson listening, occasionally nodding, and a grimace beginning to form, the grimace becoming fully formed, then gradually deepening. When she did speak, it was again in a tone that would have carried to the sitting room on the landing above.

"No, Inspector, it's not possible right now. ... I will, of course, fully inform Mr. 'Olmes when 'e gets back. ... I'll be there tomorrow to tell you what 'e suggests.... As early as I can. ... I don't know either, Inspector. .... Yes, Inspector, 'is time is quite taken up with workin' on Dr. Watson. ... I'll certainly let 'im know, Inspector, and I'm sure 'e'll appreciate it."

She came away from the phone, grimace still in place, as she faced her two colleagues. "I'm afraid we've run into a small complication. Mrs. Lestrade is returnin' 'ome."

For the better part of the next half hour, the roast that was to be their dinner sat unattended while Mrs. Hudson and her colleagues discussed the latest crisis involving the suffragettes.

Chapter 4.
A House Divided

Detective Inspector Lestrade was beginning to regret retirement. He was now faced with a challenge that dwarfed those with which he had had to contend at the Yard. Mrs. Lestrade, having decided that her mother was now much improved and able to take care of herself, had cut short her time away and was hurrying to be with him, certain of his need for a woman's presence and unaware he already had the presence of two women. Moreover, he was certain his son, a member of the Metropolitan Police constabulary, would join them as soon as he learned of his mother's return, at which time he would discover his father was harboring two fugitives from justice and had only recently released a third.

And now, after a hugely unsatisfactory telephone call, in which he was again unable to speak to Mr. Holmes, he was given to understand that, if he was to get any assistance in resolving the dilemma from the man he saw as having had a big hand in creating it, that support would be relayed to him by the man's landlady. It was true, he had to admit, that on several occasions she had seemed quite capable, but she was certainly no Sherlock Holmes. It would be a point for later discussion, but for now he had two women to dispatch as soon as possible to a location yet to be determined.

As he anticipated, his daughter, Millicent, was of no help in finding an alternative place for the suffragettes to stay. She pointed out, not unreasonably, that if she called her friends as he suggested, word would inevitably get out about "the oppressed women," as she had taken to calling their guests, and not only would the oppressed women be captured, but his family would be put at risk for what she supposed was called "abetting criminal behavior or some such thing." She reminded him—as if reminding was needed—that his son was himself a member of the Metropolitan Police. Having shared her view of the situation, Millicent went upstairs to rejoin the oppressed women she now counted as friends, if not role models. On learning of the difficulty their presence was causing, the two women came downstairs to tell Lestrade they were prepared to leave and take their chances with the authorities rather than create any further difficulty for his family.

Lestrade was briefly tempted, but ultimately unable to send the two women, little older than Millicent, out to an unknown, but surely unkind fate. "No, you'll stay the night. Tomorrow morning I'll be meeting with Mr. Holmes's … person, Mrs. Hudson, who you already know, and we'll see what action he suggests. If history is any judge, he'll have something useful to suggest. You should get a good night's sleep. It's been a long day, and we'll face tomorrow, tomorrow."

"Thank you, inspector. Thank you for this and for all the kindness you and Millicent have shown," Christabel Pankhurst spoke while Annie Kenney nodded vigorous affirmation of all she said. "And if things can't be worked out by your Mr. Holmes, we remain ready to take our leave." With that, the suffragettes and Millicent went back upstairs while Lestrade inspected the downstairs for any evidence of disarray before Mrs. Lestrade arrived home.

He achieved a reasonable measure of success such that when Mrs. Lestrade arrived, everything on the ground floor was as it should be, even as nothing on the floor above was. In any event, it had been decided that Lestrade would explain the situation to his wife before the additions to her household could be discovered. After first exchanging hugs and kisses for himself and the patiently waiting Millicent, receiving assurances regarding the health of his mother-in-law, and learning that the trip was not as taxing as Mrs. Lestrade thought it might be, it became time to describe the changed circumstances of their home.

"We've run into something of a sticky situation while you were away, dear. I've often spoken to you of Sherlock Holmes and his colleague, Dr. John Watson, and you know the regard I have for both those men. While you were gone, a man was killed, and Dr. Watson was being sought for his murder. I was certain of Dr. Watson's innocence and so I allowed him to stay here briefly until Mr. Holmes located a place for him to stay long-term."

Mrs. Lestrade seized on the moment her husband paused to catch his breath to react to what he'd said. "Well, thank goodness, he's gone. I wish the man no ill will, but can you imagine the difficulty if he was discovered in our house what with him being wanted by the police and Noah being on the police force." She gave a small shudder as she contemplated the disaster she believed to have been averted.

In concert with a groan from Millicent, Lestrade began to describe the disaster that had not been averted. "I'm afraid there's more to it, dear. You see, there were—there are—two other people—two young women—who've gotten themselves into difficulty with the authorities and who we're housing temporarily while Mr. Holmes works out a long-term solution to their problem. They're two young women who got themselves mixed up in this suffragette activity. They claim they were doing nothing more than marching when someone did some rock-throwing and they got swept up with people who were actually breaking the law. In the confusion, they managed to get away with the help of Mr. Holmes's landlady. There seemed to be no place where they could go without being arrested so I agreed that if Mr. Holmes took Watson, we'd keep the women temporarily. Of course, Millicent has been with me throughout the time the women have been here." He added the last without taking a breath between sentences, believing the women's unchaperoned stay at their home to be the more sensitive issue addressed.

"I've told these two people that, with your coming home, we need to take immediate action regarding their living arrangements. I'll be meeting with Mr. Holmes's landlady tomorrow morning to find out what Mr. Holmes has been able to come up with. That means, I'm afraid, we'll have to house the two ladies tonight. But I promise you, it will be just the one night and then out they go." Having established a framework allowing them to be rid of the intruders without sounding unfeeling for their situation, he anticipated receiving his wife's gratitude if not applause. He received neither.

No one who knew Mrs. Lestrade would describe her as a formidable woman. For one thing, her height was against it. She was no taller than Mrs. Hudson, although less matronly in appearance. She had a high forehead and small slightly hooked nose, but those were countered by bright brown eyes and a bow-like mouth that allowed her to be described as cute even as the passing years might have dictated otherwise. Now, the high forehead became the site for multiple furrows and the bow-like mouth became a tight thin line. It was not a frequent occurrence but happened often enough to alert Lestrade to prepare himself for a difficult time. When she spoke again, it became apparent that it could be a very difficult time.

"Mr. Lestrade, are you telling me that if your Mr. Holmes can't solve the problem, it's your intention to put these poor lambs out on the street to suffer whatever fate has in store for them." Lestrade was about to interrupt his wife to point out the parallels between the two women's situation and that facing Dr. Watson, but gave it up with the realization there was nothing he could say that would allow Watson to achieve poor lamb status.

"You've said yourself they were doing nothing but marching, which I believe is their perfect right to do." Her position made clear, her voice lost much of its stridency even as a harsh squint now joined the furrows in her forehead. "I've never known you to refuse help to those in need, Mr. Lestrade, but if it's your plan to start doing so now, I can tell you, you'll be sleeping alone in the future—in fact, you'll be doing a great many things alone."

While Lestrade contemplated a lonely, if quiet future, Millicent, delighted to have found a strong ally, lost no time in making her own position clear while studiously avoiding the term "poor lambs" to characterize their guests.

"You must meet these two women, mother. You'll see they are pleasant, law-abiding young ladies who are the victims of an unfair and oppressive system. They were simply marching for the right to vote when they were taken into custody by the police."

"I agree these women are hardly desperate criminals," Lestrade began, thinking it past time to defend his position. "If they were, I would never have agreed to their staying here even briefly. Nor, I'm sure, would Mr. Holmes have asked it of me. I would only point out that, whatever we think of these women, they are fugitives, and we are breaking the law in housing them. If we are found to be shielding them from the authorities, we would, at minimum, have a great deal of explaining to do and it could be far worse than that. I assure you the police do not take into consideration good intentions, but only whether a crime has been committed, and harboring fugitives is a crime. I suggest we wait to learn Mr. Holmes's thinking as to how we can protect the women without breaking the law," adding under his breath, "if that's possible."

"Let us then wait until tomorrow and see what your Mr. Holmes recommends," Mrs. Lestrade agreed, then added, "In the meantime, you may carry my case to our bedroom." The request was accompanied by a small smile that considerably lightened the burden he'd been assigned.

Millicent bounded up the stairs in front of her father to bring her two militant suffragettes downstairs to meet her mother, to whom she was certain they would appear quite lamblike.

Early the following morning, the plan, purportedly devised by Holmes, was relayed to Lestrade by its author. The inspector asked Mrs. Hudson to convey his appreciation to Mr. Holmes for "as usual working out an ingenious solution to a terribly thorny problem." The plan was shared with Mrs. Lestrade, Millicent, and her near apoplectic brother, Noah, who had come by to see his mother, and had then been introduced to the two suffragettes for whom his colleagues were searching. Nonetheless, all agreed to abide by the plan all but one found to be ingenious. By mid-morning the plan, now credited to both Holmes and Lestrade, had been adopted by the Metropolitan Police with thanks, but without comment as to its ingenious nature.

The plan was, in fact, a simple one. When arrested and briefly jailed, Mrs. Hudson couldn't help becoming aware of the terrible overcrowding at the Bow Street Station and had been led to believe that the number of demonstrators for the vote, and their willingness to become guests of the Crown on behalf of the Cause, had resulted in a dearth of accommodations throughout London's detention facilities. The situation was further complicated by the fact that the city's detention facilities had been designed with a male clientele in mind and did not address the needs of its suddenly female population. Moreover, some of that new clientele were the daughters of wealthy and politically powerful men. Thus, when Lestrade offered to place two of the women under house arrest, whereby he and his son would take full responsibility for their detention until their day in court, that offer was warmly and rapidly embraced without question raised as to how the women found their way to Lestrade's home or how long they'd been there.

The two detainees insisted that now, in light of their assignment to the Lestrade household, they be allowed to take on household duties. Mrs. Lestrade and Millicent were inclined to treat them as family members with privileges— which was to say very light household duties—while Lestrade, somewhat grudgingly, came to regard them as guests of the family. Only Noah insisted on continuing to see them as lawbreakers and thereby undeserving of any consideration other than those consistent with Metropolitan Police rules and regulations.

With the Lestrades' home having been officially designated a detention facility, Mrs. Hudson and Holmes were free to return to interrogating all who had attended Dr. Watson's dinner. The next guest on their list, Cyril Worthington, was staying at a hotel. A telegram was sent requesting his availability later that morning. Worthington's response assured his availability at eleven together with a statement of his need to be elsewhere in the early afternoon, thereby making clear he was prepared to be helpful within the limits he sought to impose.

Holmes and Mrs. Hudson arrived at the townhouse hotel where Worthington was staying a few minutes before eleven and, after a brief exchange with the assistant manager regarding respect for guests' privacy (all were in strong support of it), and protection from undesirable intruders (which the assistant manager could see they were not), he informed them of Cyril Worthington's room number and wished them a pleasant day.

Worthington proved to be tall, nearly as tall as Holmes, with a moon-shaped face that seemed out of place with his trim, muscular build. What captured Mrs. Hudson's attention, however, was what Watson had described as "his seeming to be in perpetually good humor." The crinkling at the corners of eyes that seemed determined to twinkle made clear this was a man who looked to life with a smile—whether life deserved it or not. Playing the good host, he had procured a tray of nuts, cheeses, and fruit together with a pitcher of spring water and glasses.

Amid introductions, he apologized for the water, indicating that between the hour and his ignorance of their tastes, water seemed the safest choice. Both Holmes and Mrs. Hudson protested that water was fine and the tray he provided was a delightful surprise. He invited them to take the two chairs that stood to one side of the room's small table while he took the easy chair that stood to its other side. With the pleasantries disposed of, it was time for the questioning to begin.

Holmes took the lead. "You were seated very near to the victim, Mr. Worthington. Looking back, do you recall seeing anything that you would now say appeared suspicious?"

"You mean like someone putting cyanide in Reggie's wine glass?"

"And how would you know about the cyanide?"

"It's not because I'm a murderer, Mr. Holmes. It's because I read the *Morning Standard*. See for yourself." With that, he handed the newspaper to Holmes who had, in fact, seen the headline but not read the story, choosing instead to scan the paper's "agony" column in the time available before leaving 221B.

Holmes passed the paper to Mrs. Hudson, who had read the news story earlier that morning, then continued his questioning.

"And did you see anyone put cyanide in Mr. Miles's wine glass?"

"Of course not. For one thing, I wouldn't know what was or wasn't cyanide, but I didn't see anybody put anything in Reggie's wine glass. You do know, I assume, that we were all out of the dining room for a while looking at Dr. Watson's photographs, with the glasses for port on the table in the other room and people strolling in and out of the study. And, before you ask, that includes me who had need of the privy—begging your pardon, ma'am—but I suppose you need to know."

"Can you tell us who you saw leave the study durin' the time you were lookin' at photographs?" The question was posed in a Cockney accent that led Worthington to adopt a brief look of surprise before resetting the small smile he had been wearing.

"I'll try ma'am but monitoring use of the ... facilities was not something of great interest to me so my list will almost certainly be incomplete."

Mrs. Hudson blushed her own small smile. "I understand, Mr. Worthington. Just tell us what you remember."

"Well then, there was Mr. Clark. I remember him because he excused himself to get a smoke, but he left with his wife which I thought was sort of odd because I couldn't figure her for smoking in public. In private either come to that. And he didn't come back with her, which, of course, he would have done if they had stayed together. And I remember Wilson James because he had been sitting next to me before he got up and changed seats like I had body odor or something. Besides which, he looked to me like someone who might steal the silverware, so I sort of kept an eye on him. That's all I can say definitely—anyway, of the men but I'm sure there were others. I remember seeing Violet leaving the same time as Mrs. Clark. I was curious about that, and I do know Violet a long time, so I asked her what it was all about, and she told me after that she and Mrs. Clark wanted to refamiliarize themselves with the house and see what changes had been made since their last visits. Funny thing about it, though, they didn't come back together like I would've expected.

"And, of course, like everyone else I kept an eye on Reginald ... Reggie. Mostly, he just sat and watched while Dr. Watson explained about his photographs. He didn't himself go near Dr. Watson, which I personally was glad to see since it was obvious at the dinner there was bad blood between them. Anyway, the two of them both went out of the study at one point—or really at two points since they definitely didn't leave together."

"And you said that you also left the study at one point?" Holmes asked.

"I did, yes. What of it?"

"Perhaps nothing. I simply want to be certain our record of people's comings and goings is accurate." With that, Holmes made a small show of writing in the accounts book he had borrowed from Watson.

Mrs. Hudson took advantage of the silence between the two men to turn the discussion to another area she wanted to explore. Recalling Watson's description of Worthington, she asked, "Would I be correct in sayin' that other than family, you'd known Mr. Miles longer than anyone else at the dinner?"

Worthington showed a cautious smile as he answered Mrs. Hudson's question. "Yes, ma'am, in fact it's only his sister, Violet, who knows him longer."

"And that means you knew him from before he married Natalie?" Worthington winced slightly, before giving enough of a nod to allow Mrs. Hudson to continue questioning and to wonder at Worthington's reaction to the woman's name.

"And I'm supposin' that given 'ow long ago all that was, you knew him when he was goin' on 'is gamblin' trips."

It was a statement, not a question and was followed with a second statement camouflaged as a question. "And bein' that you were a good friend, it likely means you shared some of the same interests and so you likely went with 'im on some of those gamblin' trips? Maybe more than some."

Cyril Worthington straightened in his seat, the smile gone, he had a question that was a question.

"What do you know of Reggie's habits?"

"I know when someone is gone from his family for long periods and sometimes comes 'ome well off and more often not so well off—like they say was the case with Mr. Miles—'e likely 'as the gamblin' bug, which can be awfully 'ard to get rid of. And the fact that you used to travel with 'im, and don't any longer, means you did get rid of the bug, but Mr. Miles didn't."

"You're right, ma'am, anyway on most of it. When you quit your own gambling, you want to get as far from temptation as you possibly can. I didn't want to see Reggie or hear from him. But there was more to it than that. Reggie came to be a leech. Which is to say if you gave him half a chance, he'd attach himself to you and never let go—anyway not as long as you had any money he thought he might get from you. Of course, I knew what that was like, having been there myself. But never as bad as Reggie. He'd think he had a hot tip and he'd sell his soul to make the bet and, if you'd give it to him, he'd take your last shilling, promising to pay you back as soon as he collected his winnings. Except most times there wasn't any winnings, or if there was, there were so many people to pay back, you could be a long time waiting your turn. Anyway, because I knew what it was like and how giving Reggie an inch would lead to him trying to take a mile, I stopped seeing him a long time ago. At least I did up until this one time about two weeks ago when he contacted me and he sounded so desperate that I agreed to meet with him. I did set one condition. I told him I'd only see him if he promised in advance that he wouldn't ask me for any money. Not that that kind of promise would mean much to Reggie, but I got to say, he held to it.

"As it turned out, what he wanted was advice, or really maybe just to talk. He said he didn't have anybody else who would understand or that he wouldn't be ashamed to tell. That's when he told me he'd been getting money from loan sharks and was maybe getting in over his head, except the more he talked, the more you could tell there was no 'maybe' about it. He wanted to know if I had any contacts from the old days who could meet with these guys on his behalf and maybe buy him some time or whatever. Of course, like I was saying, I'm completely out of that life and there was nothing I could do for him. And then, just like that, he's back to same old Reggie, I shouldn't worry, he tells me, he's got a sure-fire way of getting even. But he does ask me to keep quiet about his situation and, in fact, the two of you are the only people I've told." Worthington winced as he considered the dilemma his one-time friend faced. "When all was said and done, Reggie wasn't the worst I've known. He just couldn't let loose of the bug."

He put on a crooked smile and looked to his visitors. "Is any of this helpful to you? I'm afraid there's nothing I know of that gets your friend off the hook."

"I would say you've been of considerable help, Mr. Worthington. You've mentioned at least four people beside yourself who would have had access to Mr. Miles's wine glass with no one present, except possibly a confederate," Holmes observed drily. "And you've brought up these people called loan sharks. It's certainly important we know about them. You've also suggested there are a number of people who could have felt resentful about being used by Miles in terms of lending him money with no likelihood of their ever being paid back. On that score, we know from others that Mr. Miles didn't shrink from threatening people he knew, even people with whom he'd been friends, with the exposure of things they'd find embarrassing or worse if they didn't '*lend*' him money.

"Whoa! Just hold on there, Mr. Holmes, you should know he didn't try to pull anything like that with me. I didn't say nothin' like that. I admit, I did lend him money early on when I didn't know any better, but he had nothing to hold over my head. Nothing." At the last "nothing" Worthington got to his feet. "I think that's all I've got to say on the subject and it's not like you're with the police and I've got to answer your questions, so I suggest we end it here and we both get on with our days." To make certain his statement was understood, Worthington rose from his chair with eyes narrowly focused on Holmes and Mrs. Hudson making the tacit demand they do the same.

Holmes and Mrs. Hudson proceeded to the hotel room door, by now accustomed to wearing out their welcome not long after its being proffered. Holmes lingered on the threshold long enough to call back some words of advice. "You should prepare yourself, Mr. Worthington. We may well be back—and the police may have questions of their own."

Once outside, it occurred to Holmes and Mrs. Hudson they had eaten nothing from the tray Worthington provided and were now very hungry.

They returned to 221B for a quick bite "to tide them over" as Holmes described it. The quick bite consisted of tea and the scones that had come out of the oven shortly before the morning's visit to Worthington. While they ate, they shared with Watson a detailed account of that visit. They hoped to provide Watson the material for another of his popular tales that, like those that had come before, would speak with admiration of Holmes's incisiveness and analytic ability, and speak not at all of Mrs. Hudson. Neither questioned the certainty both felt that Watson would be with them to write the tale.

Before leaving to meet with the Johnsons, Margaret's sister, Violet, and her husband, Stanford, Watson thought it wise to remind Holmes and Mrs. Hudson that Violet very much disliked and distrusted Reginald Miles and disagreed strongly with her sister about his willingness or capacity for change. She had, in fact, largely stopped visiting their home on that account. He was sure the animosity Violet felt for her brother was shared by her husband and, in truth, his own feelings about Reginald had become something of a sore point between himself and Margaret. Mrs. Hudson suggested that his feelings toward Reginald Miles appeared widely shared, but that he should, nonetheless, not volunteer the fact that he was one of the sharers.

The modesty of the Johnson home came as a surprise to Holmes and Mrs. Hudson. They judged there were no more than two rooms down, excluding the kitchen, and three on the floor above. Mrs. Hudson speculated that Violet Johnson was likely none too pleased with the disbursement of funds from her father's estate. While her sister, Margaret, seemed in need of support as a lone widow with a meager inheritance from her husband, Violet appeared to enjoy only a small advantage over her sister, an advantage that disappeared with Margaret's second marriage.

Violet had been watching for her visitors and came out on the porch to greet them, calling to her husband that their company had arrived. He joined her on the porch, and the four of them went briefly through introductions before the Johnsons ushered Holmes and Mrs. Hudson into what Holmes would later describe as a "sitting room, largely because there was nothing but sitting that could be done there." There were three armed easy chairs and a couch. All four pieces were of oak, and all had the same pale blue cushions. A low table completed the ensemble. To Mrs. Hudson's eye, the Johnsons's furnishings appeared adequate but paled in comparison to the Clarks's furnishings and, though giving every indication of being carefully tended, they nonetheless showed the nicks and scratches inevitable with age. As if to compensate for the leaden feel of the room's furniture, a layering of shelves in every corner of the room gave rise to a virtual fleet of ships permanently moored in a collection of bottles. Mrs. Hudson judged that Stanford Johnson, the banker, carried over the attention to detail practiced during his days at the bank to the hobby he had adopted for his evenings at home. Recognition of Mr. Johnson's skills seemed to Mrs. Hudson a useful and appropriate strategy for gaining the Johnsons's cooperation for the tasks ahead.

"I'm admirin' what I believe to be your ship-building skills, Mr. Johnson." She beamed her admiration to Johnson and was rewarded with a bashful smile from the craftsman, and words of appreciation from Violet Johnson.

"Stanford is too modest to say it, so I will. This is only part of his collection. There's lots more upstairs. There's also the prizes he's won and an article from the *Morning Standard* written a little over a year ago that tells about his ships in bottles and about Stanford. I'll tell you this: if we ever had a fire—God forbid—I don't know if Stanford would look to save me or his collection."

"I guess I'm like everybody else in not knowin' 'ow they get the boats with all their masts in the little bottles." Mrs. Hudson was determined to milk all the good will she could manage before broaching questions likely to engender ill will. Stanford Johnson was aware his visitors had not come solely to admire his ship-building skills and felt it time to address the reason they had come.

"It's very good of you to take recognition of my work—I do appreciate it—but we know you're here on a far more serious mission than to admire my ships. You have question about my brother-in-law's death, and, I feel certain, about the role my other brother-in-law, Dr. Watson, played in his death. We have nothing to hide, Mr. Holmes. You can ask whatever you wish."

"Thank you, Mr. Johnson," Holmes attempted to maintain the conciliatory spirit begun by Mrs. Hudson. "In that vein, Mr. Johnson, Mrs. Johnson, can you tell me if you saw anything you felt to be suspicious or questionable at any time during the evening?"

"You mean apart from Reginald falling dead across the table?" Johnson alone found his quip amusing and so made a gesture of waving away any notion his audience might have that he was not taking things as seriously as he should. Violet groaned, suggesting to Mrs. Hudson that such comments from her husband were not entirely novel. His follow-up observation confirmed Mrs. Hudson's suspicion about the many-sided bank clerk.

"One thing that I find puzzling is why it took so long for somebody to kill him—especially given the people at Watson's dinner party." Violet, having done what she could to control her husband through disapproving looks and soft groans, now turned to speech in a seemingly doomed effort to keep him in check.

"Really, Stanford, you'll have our guests thinking we all joined together to kill Reginald."

Johnson showed his wife a mischievous grin. "That's a good idea or would have been if you had suggested it earlier."

Mrs. Hudson seized on Johnson's flippant remark to explore his thinking about Dr. Watson's dinner guests. "Are you sayin' that the several people around the table 'ad their own grievances with Mr. Miles?"

"I'm saying exactly that?"

Holmes, taking his cue from Mrs. Hudson, reentered the conversation. "Could you elaborate on that, Mr. Johnson."

"There are no secrets between sisters, Mr. Holmes—anyway no secrets about people other than themselves, and not many between a husband and wife—not in a good marriage." Stanford Johnson smiled broadly to his wife who managed a tentative smile in return as she waited to learn what secrets her husband was about to reveal.

"And you probably know that Reginald Miles was highly skilled at borrowing but a total failure when it came to paying back. And if he knew anything about you that could be embarrassing—or worse—he had no compunction about using whatever he had found out to demand a loan that he never intended to pay back. He tried it on me—just once, mind you. He found out about my getting arrested as a boy for stealing fruit from a costermonger's cart. And with my working in the bank, it looked like that would be something I'd want to hide—and so would *loan* him some money to keep it hid. Except that I didn't. I thought about it alright, I'll say that. But I figured if I once got started down that road, there'd likely be no turning back.

"Instead, I told Reginald I wouldn't pay him a single shilling and he could do what he liked about it. Of course, I only did that after first telling Mr. Benedict, the bank manager, about my arrest. Well, Mr. Benedict made it clear that, what with my years of loyal service and unblemished record, he was totally uninterested in what he called my 'boyhood indiscretion.' He also said he was gonna forget I told him about it and that I should forget about it too. Which I have done until now, Mr. Holmes.

"Well, when Reginald found out he wasn't getting any money from me, he lost all interest in my boyhood arrest in spite of his threat. At least I never heard anything further about it and I'm sure I would have if he told anyone."

Holmes nodded appreciation for Johnson's confession and attempted to expand on it. "Do you believe there were others at the dinner who had been approached by Miles or were already paying him for his silence?"

"I'm sorry, Mr. Holmes. I don't think it's my place to name names; I'll just say it wouldn't surprise me."

"What is it that you want from us, Mr. Holmes?" Violet asked in a voice that made clear her frustration. "I just don't see how we can be helpful. We didn't see or hear anything different from what anybody else did. I know that Mrs. Clark told you that she and I met up after leaving the study where Dr. Watson was showing his photographs, and Stanford left the study at one point as well, but it was all very innocent. I wanted to see what the house looked like with my sister gone and Mrs. Clark had the same idea; and Stanford had need of the facilities. And that's all there is to it. I suppose you're wondering about the inheritance from my sister's passing. It's no secret we are in line for some money but only after Dr. Watson has passed away—and honestly, neither Stanford nor I are that grasping that we would ever want it to come to that."

"It is one of the several ways we choose to separate ourselves from Reginald." Stanford Johnson fairly shook with rage as he recounted the depth of his feelings toward his brother-in-law. "You must understand the depravity of the man. Violet and I were able to escape his clumsy attempt at blackmail, I have reason to believe others were not. And these were people who had once been his friends and colleagues. It was his treatment of Cyril all over again."

The room went suddenly silent but for another groan from Violet. It was left to Mrs. Hudson to follow up as casually and in as soft a tone as she could manage. "Could you tell us please, Mr. Johnson, what you mean by his treatment of Mr. Worthington all over again."

The Johnsons looked to each other, Mr. Johnson shame-faced and Violet Johnson with resignation. It was Violet who spoke to the issue her husband had surfaced and gave him license to pursue it. "I'm afraid the cat's out of the bag, Stanford. You might as well tell them."

Stanford gave a reluctant nod but sought assurances before telling what he knew. "I need you to regard what I'm going to tell you as deeply confidential. It's something that's known by most of us in the family and by no one outside the family—and we'd like it to stay that way." He looked hard to Holmes and Mrs. Hudson, neither of whom gave an immediate response. Mrs. Hudson thought it wise to provide him a part of the reassurance he obviously felt was lacking.

"You must understand, Mr. Johnson, we are conductin' an investigation of murder. We are not 'ere wantin' to deal in gossip. What you tell us will be treated with the greatest respect. If it is seen as important to our investigation—and only if it is seen as important to our investigation—we will make use of it while respectin' the confidentiality of all those involved, includin', of course, those who made us aware of the information." That said, Mrs. Hudson sat back and watched Johnson's face as he screwed it into a look of intense concentration before beginning an uncharacteristically carefully considered explanation.

"I will then depend on your discretion. It's well known that there came to be bad blood between Reginald and his one-time friend, Cyril Worthington. What's not so well known is that the bad blood's got nothing to do with money which is what people think. The real cause of the trouble had to do with Natalie, Reginald's wife. See, it was all very hush, hush, but before she got involved with Reginald, Cyril was sure she'd be marching down the aisle with him. He maybe should have guessed something when she told him she didn't want him to tell anybody about them being a couple for a while. She had it in mind for him to say they were just good friends.

Well, Cyril had to tell somebody his news, and he and Violet always had a special relationship, so we ended up knowing, but it was just us and on condition we say nothing to anyone else. Which we pretty nearly done. The trouble is when things were going well for Cyril, we wanted to share the good news with somebody ourselves. So, we ended up telling Margaret, knowing she'd be happy for Cyril, and knowing, as well, that she could keep a secret. Of course, then, when things didn't turn out the way we all hoped, we had to share that with Margaret as well.

We think that's one of the reasons she wanted Cyril at the dinner party. The other is, of course, that Cyril is an old friend of the family. But I'm sure Margaret was thinking that, with all the time that's passed, with Natalie gone and with the friendship that used to be, there was a fair chance that Reginald and Cyril could make up with each other. And she could have been right. Cyril seemed to be okay, even chipper at the dinner. Of course, no one spoke Natalie's name so there's no telling if that would have set sparks flying. Anyway, that's the whole of it, Mr. Holmes, and, as I said, I'd appreciate the both of you keeping what I've told you to yourselves." There were grunted acknowledgments of his request but nothing that could be taken as a commitment. Instead, Mrs. Hudson thought to step up the interrogation.

"Thank you for sharin' that, Mr. Johnson. I need to ask you about one other thing we've been told. It's our understandin' that your Aunt Margaret's will provides for her fortune to go to her sister, Violet, and her brother, Reginald. Of course, with Reginald gone, and Edward 'is only son, it seems certain that 'e and Alice will be given the share that was to come to Reginald. And with Mr. Miles now gone and Dr. Watson seemingly about to be, there's nothin' to keep your inheritances from goin' through.

84

"Well, you can see how that might look to the police, what with the two people who stood in the way of your inheritin' your sister's fortune both gotten rid of in the same evenin'. There'll be questions, of course, and you will want to be ready for them. Somebody should probably let the Mileses know to be ready as well. You can see 'ow just lookin' at the facts, one could think the both of you could have worked together to get to the inheritance or, of course, either one of you could 'ave acted alone."

Stanford Johnson stared, for the moment open-mouthed and speechless, then closed-mouthed but still speechless. Violet Johnson had speech enough for them both.

"If you're saying what I think you're saying, Mrs. Hudson, it's a monstrous thing to suggest. Have you asked Edward the same question about his inheritance?" While daggers shone from Violet Johnson's eyes, Mrs. Hudson's expression never changed as she waited the protestation of innocence, she was certain would be forthcoming. That protestation turned out to be liberally mixed with indignation.

"Is this your thinking as well, Mr. Holmes? Do you think Stanford and I murdered my brother, or maybe colluded with my nephew to commit murder to get at the family's inheritance?" She looked for the moment to Holmes, then continued without waiting for a response.

"Is it also what the police believe? Can anyone tell me how we worked it out? Was it my idea or Edward's ... or maybe Alice is the evil genius?" She gave a brief shudder on hearing her own creation. "I've never been so insulted, and in my own house yet."

Stanford Johnson judged his wife had shared the last of her indignation and it was now time for him to bring the visit to an end. "I believe you've gotten from us all that we have to share. Now, we need to get on with our day. You're not the police and I'd be obliged if you'd get on with your day as well" He stood at the last and waited for his guests to do likewise.

Holmes and Mrs. Hudson edged off of their chairs, affecting a reluctance to leave that neither felt. Violet remained seated, unwilling to exhibit anything approaching grace as she took her leave of them. Her husband saw them to the door, where he wordlessly nodded his good-bye as they exited into a sunlit day whose warm glow was in sharp contrast to the climate they had just left.

Holmes and Mrs. Hudson agreed to hold off discussion of their visit with the Mileses until Watson could join them later. To make certain no essential items would go unreported, they independently recorded their recollections of the more significant events each had witnessed. With those papers safely tucked away for later use, and the sun still high in the heavens, it was deemed well to visit the last of Watson's guests before returning to Baker Street. They had the address at which Wilson James maintained offices as a property agent in Lambeth and judged the nature of his business would cause him to be there at this hour of the day. They knew as well that once he and Reginald Miles had been partners, and that the reason they broke up was—again, according to Watson—a secret everyone described as best left unexplored.

As Holmes opened the door to W. W. James, property manager, a bell above the door sounded his and Mrs. Hudson's arrival with a loud, if unharmonious tinkling. James sat behind a desk facing the door allowing him to give each prospective client the welcoming smile that now wreathed his face as they entered his offices. As Mrs. Hudson became visible from behind Holmes's back, the smile impossibly broadened as he rose from behind his desk to give the warmest possible greeting. Couples were, after all, far more likely to lead to a sale than a man or woman alone.

James was, in every part, a middle-aged man in the thick of battle against being middle-aged. He was portly, not yet fat, but well on his way to that unwanted objective. Once thick sandy brown hair was now grey, and grey hair was combed over an ever-expanding patch without hair of any color. A small squint revealed his nearsightedness—corrected as needed by the rimless glasses that lay at the ready on a corner of his desk. As surreptitiously as he could, he studied what appeared to him an unusual couple—a woman not quite old enough to be the man's mother but almost certainly too old to be his wife. Still, he'd been in business long enough to be prepared for nearly anything.

"Good afternoon. Is there some way I can be of service? Are you perhaps thinking of acquiring property in the Lambeth area? If you are, you couldn't have come at a better time. Some truly choice property has come on the market at very competitive prices." He stopped talking but maintained the smile as he waved them to two chairs at a table to their right on which were stacked books presumably containing descriptions of the choice property that had come on the market. Holmes and Mrs. Hudson thought it advisable to make clear the nature of their business.

"Thank you, Mr. James. Before we go any farther, I need to explain to you who we are and the nature of our business." The detectives noted that, as expected, the smile melted away and James now directed them to the two chairs on the opposite side of the desk from where he now reseated himself.

"You may have heard of me. I'm Sherlock Holmes. The lady with me is Mrs. Hudson, and we are investigating the death of Reginald Miles. In that regard, we are interviewing all the people who were guests at the dinner party at which Miles was poisoned."

"I don't understand, Mr. Holmes. It was my understanding that the police thought it certain they had got their man—this bloke, Watson—and it was just a matter of finding him after he ran off—pretty much establishing his guilt I would think. Have the police changed their mind? Is that why you're here? Are you helping them out?"

"We're definitely helping them out although sort of unofficially. It's something we do all the time. We have the capacity to look at things a little differently than they do, and we can then share our observations and conclusions with them where that seems appropriate." Aware that a client could appear at any time, Holmes attempted to expedite the proceedings, "You're a busy man and it would be well for us to get started. I believe you sat between Watson and the Johnsons at the dinner at which Reginald Miles was poisoned?"

James nodded cautiously.

"Did you see anything you regarded as suspicious or simply inappropriate from where you sat?"

"No, I can't say I did."

"And when you went to the other room to look at Watson's photographs of his trip with his wife, did you see anything you would term suspicious there?"

"No, I can't say I saw anything out of the ordinary there either. Of course, you could say that all of us having to move into the other room because of things getting a little rough was out of the ordinary, but I'm sure you know all about that from the others you've talked to by now."

Mrs. Hudson spoke to James's assumption. "People can see the same things very differently. Tell us, if you would, 'ow you saw the need to move to the other room."

"To my mind, it was inevitable. I mean things getting rough and us having to get away from the table. You combine people—none of them with what you could call a fondness for Miles and some of them with a real dislike for the man— with a seemingly endless supply of wine and eventually things are going to give way. Which is what happened. I don't know how it got started, but it was like here we were one minute breaking bread together all nice and peaceful and the next minute we're hinting around about how we really feel about Miles, with some of us maybe doing more than just hinting. And, for that matter, with Miles saying some rough things about Watson. But, other than that, don't ask me who said what because that's all jumbled up in my mind."

James's face had increasingly reddened, and his voice sounded increasingly throaty as he labored to keep his own feelings under control. Mrs. Hudson spoke to that difficulty.

"Was your voice one of those sayin' 'ow you feel'?"

"It was. I won't deny it. I had my own reasons for having no use for Miles. Still and all, I had met his sister, Margaret, on several occasions and I liked her, so when I heard she was the one who wanted me there, I put my feelings about her brother to one side—or tried to, at least for the evening."

Holmes followed up James's acknowledgment of a problem. "Tell us, if you would please, the reason for your feelings."

"It's not something I'm proud of. Do we really need to talk about it?" The question was directed to Holmes but was answered in a Cockney accent.

"I'm afraid we do. A man is dead. A man with enemies, several of whom were in the room where he was poisoned. The police have arrested Dr. Watson, but there are questions even with Mr. Miles apparently accusin' 'im. For one thing, nobody saw Dr. Watson put poison in Mr. Miles's glass. It's that kind of thing that's certain to get the police to look further and to look at things like people's motives— which is to say why they had angry feelings towards Mr. Miles. We're just tryin' to get an understandin' of all that and make sure the right person is charged with the crime. And, of course, we want to do that as quickly as possible, 'opefully, before the police come around with a bunch of questions that maybe get the story into the dailies with whatever that does to people and their businesses."

In spite of an initial difficulty with the woman's dialect, her message was quickly grasped by Wilson James. "I'll tell you about Miles and me, but I ask you to treat what I tell you with the discretion it deserves. My problems with him started seven years ago—seven years and two months which is when my wife first got sick. We had hopes for her recovery, but the treatment was very expensive. Way beyond our means. You've got to understand. Everyday I'm watching the woman I love move a step closer to death and there's nothing I can do about it because I haven't got the money. Me, who's supposed to be the provider, who's supposed to be my wife's protector. Well, I figured out what I had to do. I borrowed from our account, Miles's and mine. We were property agents in business together back then. And, when all was said and done, getting the money was surprisingly easy. I was the one handling the finances and I'd just hold back for myself a part of what one client paid, then replenish his account with the money I collected from the next client, except for the money I held out from him and so on. As long as we could maintain a steady stream of clients---which we did—it could all work out.

"And you've got to understand something about Miles back then. He didn't have the gambling bug really bad when we started out. It only came on gradually and probably surprised the both of us when it took him over completely. Anyway, in the end, all my conniving and all the treatment I could buy couldn't save Jessica. And, of course, after she passed, I had no reason to borrow money from our business and I started making things right. Which was also about the time Miles developed a sudden interest in our finances. Looking back, I'd guess it had a lot to do with his gambling losses that were starting to mount up. Well, even before he looked over the books, I told him what I'd been doing and the need of it as far as I was concerned. And like I say, he was a different person back then. He said he understood; he even said he'd of done the same thing.

"Regardless, it was just a few months later, he asked if he could borrow ten pounds. At that time, he didn't say anything about the accounts. He put it on the basis of our being friends and business partners. It was only later he talked about my diddling the books and how it might look to others. He never put it in terms of buying his silence but, of course, he never had to. We both knew what was going on. By that time, we also knew we couldn't work together any longer and we went our separate ways—except for his coming to see me every now and again to borrow more money. I might not see him for several months, but, until now, I always knew he'd be back. And, of course, I knew I'd be giving him money I'd never see again." James shook his head as if trying to shake off painful memories. "At least now that nightmare is over."

Wilson James issued a lengthy sigh, then waited the judgment his confession would elicit. The woman with the Cockney accent spoke first and surprised him with the nature of her comments and the fervor with which she spoke them.

"You've been a good 'usband, Mr. James. There's none can fault you for the lengths you've gone to save your wife." Having rendered her judgment, Mrs. Hudson turned to look expectantly to Holmes.

To James's eyes it looked as though the woman he understood to be a housekeeper was directing the legendary detective's response, a turn of event he found too improbable to believe. Nonetheless, whatever the reason, the great detective fairly echoed the woman's judgment. "You did what you had to do under terribly trying circumstances. No man can fault you for that, and I am certain no woman would."

The unexpected support he received emboldened James to lay bare his concerns. "You can understand what it would do to my business if my … indiscretions became known. It's why I paid Reginald to keep silent and why I ask you to keep silent as well."

Holmes repeated his promise but now felt impelled to add a caveat. "We will, I assure you, treat what you have told us with the greatest discretion. Nonetheless, you must realize that, however justified, your actions left you open to blackmail and gave you cause to rid yourself of the blackmailer. I would urge you to prepare yourself for questions from the police while I will be doing all I can to expose the murderer as quickly as I can." Holmes smiled his most reassuring to James who tried but failed to reciprocate.

Holmes and Mrs. Hudson recognized they had exhausted their welcome, such as it was, but there was now an unsettled look on James's face. Speaking in recognition of that look, Mrs. Hudson paused before leaving her chair. "I'm wonderin' if there's anythin' else you want to tell us before we go."

"I suppose I just want it to be clear that I have … had strong feelings against the man, but if I wanted to kill Miles, I wouldn't have waited this long." He paused before adding a final thought. "If it wasn't Watson, I hope you catch whoever did it, not just to avoid my having to talk about the things I did, but for me to thank whoever it was for doing what I didn't have the courage to do myself. And I'm certain there are others who feel the same as I do."

With that, Wilson James stood, nodding his good-byes to Holmes and Mrs. Hudson as they turned to exit. There was no hint of the broad smile that had greeted them a lifetime earlier.

Chapter 5.
Constable Lestrade Makes an Impression and Is Impressed

While Holmes and Mrs. Hudson were traveling to 221B to inform Watson of the day's events, develop a plan for the next day, and somewhere between the two enjoy a leisurely dinner, Constable Noah Lestrade was traveling to his parents' home to make clear—in the strongest possible terms—his reservations about their house guests. The two women were, after all, lawbreakers and were to be treated as lawbreakers for whatever time they were living in his parents' home. In fact, according to his colleagues at the station, their crime went beyond simply breaking English law; the whole of the suffragette movement was seen as a violation of natural law, what with their talk about doing things outside the home that would make them the same as men. Although he did not agree with all aspects of their argument, it did reinforce his belief that his family did not fully understand the consequences of their well-meaning actions, and he meant to help them see the light that shone so brightly for him.

The scene that greeted Noah Lestrade on his arrival home did not augur well for the task he had set himself. His mother was filling, or more likely refilling Annie Kenney's teacup while listening intently to whatever radical proposal Christabel Pankhurst was outlining to her and an enraptured Millicent. His mother finished pouring tea, set the pot down and went to embrace her son. Millicent remained at the table along with the practitioners of civil disobedience who showed, in fact, a very civil smile and wave to the constable. Noah was not one to be put off by such obvious tactics and merely grimaced in return.

"Where's father? I need to speak with him."

"You know your father. He said he had to get away for a while," Mrs. Lestrade reported, "I suspect he's over at The Lion and The Lamb. I'm sure he'll be back in time for dinner just like always." Then, as an afterthought, "Can you stay for supper, Noah? We've more than enough and you've always liked curry."

"Besides which, if you stay you can maybe learn something." It was Millicent who extended her own version of an invitation to dinner.

Ignoring his sister as he did routinely, he gave in to the temptation posed by lamb curry. "I suppose I might just as well—if you're sure there's enough."

Mrs. Lestrade smiled her assurance.

"I wonder if I could ask a favor, Constable," Christabel Pankhurst looked hopefully to Noah.

"What kind of favor, Miss Pankhurst?"

"Really a simple one. You know that Miss Kenney and I have been confined here for the last couple of days. Don't misunderstand me, I'm eternally grateful to you and your family for the protection you've provided. And, of course, I speak for Miss Kenney in that regard as well as myself. It's just that we've been unable to go anywhere or do anything for fear of being discovered. We thought that situation might be changed with us now being under house arrest and no longer having to fear being sent to jail. I know it's not precisely what's intended, but we thought it might not be stretching the rules too much if we were to get some air with you along to maintain our supervision. It occurred to us, however, that the two of us, that is, Miss Kenney and I, might attract attention whereas just one of us walking with you wouldn't draw a second look. Miss Kenney agreed to my going first. That is, of course, if all this is agreeable to you, Constable."

Four women stared at Noah awaiting his answer. He suddenly felt an overwhelming urge to join his father at The

Lion and The Lamb. Nothing was going as he had planned. Instead of structuring the course of action his family would take with the miscreants, the miscreants were structuring the course of action he would take while his family looked on. In short order he heard himself agreeing to go for a brief outing, only stipulating that Miss Pankhurst wear the hat that best hid her features and an outfit that would draw the least possible attention. What he thought, but didn't say, was that, as a handsome woman, it would be impossible for her not to attract attention. He would rely on his uniform and helmet to achieve the inattention her outfit alone could not. What he didn't allow to surface to the level of thought was the good feeling he would enjoy from walking out with an attractive woman.

When she rejoined him, it was with a broad-brimmed hat she had pulled part way down the left side of her forehead giving greater visibility to the floral display atop the hat and less to her features beneath it. She had also put on a short jacket, ostensibly to please the constable by making her trim figure appear less trim but really to afford protection against the sudden chill in the night air. She pronounced herself ready and promised Mrs. Lestrade she'd be back to help with dinner. Millicent called, "have fun," after them, but not in a way that suggested an expectation of her wish being fulfilled.

They were past the privacy wall and had started up the empty street when Christabel decided to break what otherwise promised to be a prolonged, if not never-ending silence with a few innocuous observations.

"Your family is really very nice." Noah grunted.

"It's extremely kind of them to take in Miss Kenney and myself." A second grunt.

"Your sister has been particularly helpful." A groan.

Christabel was now of the opinion that banality, no matter how well intended, was unlikely to release a torrent of speech. She decided to take a different tack.

"I judge you don't approve of Miss Kenney and my being here. Do you also disapprove of our activity?"

Her question broke the dam and let flow a far greater torrent than she anticipated. "Of course, I don't approve of you and Miss Kenney being here. I know that everyone sees it as acceptable because of the way we're now looking at house arrest. But that won't last and maybe one of those scribblers, looking for a story, finds out you people were staying here before there was the change in house arrest, and maybe, what with my mother being big-hearted and Millicent being a muttonhead, you're still here after things have changed back. My father is retired from the Yard, but he is still a respected—highly respected—detective inspector. Do you know what it would do to his reputation if he was reported to be harboring lawbreakers? What it would do to him. And, okay, it wouldn't do me any good either, but I'm young. I could do other things if it came to that, but his reputation is all my father has."

"You do know we've offered to leave and your mother and Millicent won't hear of it. I know your father isn't pleased, but he has been an angel in continuing to protect us. We've tried to do our part, as well, staying hidden and doing what work we can around the house. Miss Kenney has been particularly good that way. Helping with the cleaning and cooking. She makes me feel positively useless."

After an initial grunt he deemed insufficient, Noah gave grudging acknowledgment of Christabel's statement. "I'm not saying you—both of you—haven't tried to be helpful."

Grudging or not, it sounded to Christabel a turn in the conversation and, never one to shrink from pressing an issue, she moved the conversation up a level. "I asked you earlier if you disapproved of Miss Kenney and my activity."

"When you break the law, absolutely I disapprove. But I know that's not what you mean. I wouldn't say I exactly disapprove. It's more like I don't see why it's necessary or appropriate. I mean women have a tough enough job. I'm talking about women like my mother—forget Millicent for the moment, although she'll probably change with time—maybe a lot of time. Anyway, with most all women, you get married and then you've got a house to run, and children to raise. With cooking and cleaning and a houseful of children, a woman would seem to have more than enough to do without trying to run the country, or anyway wanting to help pick the men that will run the country. But I'm sure that's not how you and Miss Kenney see it."

"So, if I understand you, it's not that women aren't smart enough or capable enough to be given the vote, it's that their role is different. They should be content to maintain a house and care for children."

"I didn't say anything about smart. I'd put my mother up against any man I know. And Millicent isn't stupid, she's just scattered. It's about jobs and responsibilities. Men have to do certain things and women have to do certain things. Just like it's always been."

"But not like it always has to be. Still, Constable Lestrade, you give me hope. You're not saying women lack the ability to contribute to government with their vote, you're saying it's an unfair burden. But I can tell you, Constable Lestrade, there are a great many women who would welcome just such a burden."

Whatever response Noah might have made went unspoken as suddenly and urgently, duty called. Half a street away a hansom cab was stopped. Its driver, recognizable by virtue of his somewhat battered top hat and the whip in his hand, was loudly arguing with his passenger, recognizable by virtue of his position in front of the cab's door and his jacket lapel in the firm grip of the driver's free hand, while his own hand was holding firm to the driver's arm holding the whip. After asking Christabel to wait, Noah hurried to the site of the altercation. When he was within shouting distance, he made known his presence and issued a command commensurate with that status.

"I am Constable Noah Lestrade, and I am directing you to unhand each other."

The men did not unhand each other but did relax their grips as both turned to look at the figure running toward them. They remained frozen in place until Noah arrived and gave them further instruction. "Now, let go of each other and tell me what this is all about?"

The two men dropped their hands, then entered into a simultaneous effort to advance their cause. As a consequence, neither man's cause was advanced with any clarity. To remedy the situation, Noah elected to give further direction to the situation. Pointing to the driver, he commanded, "First, your name and then your complaint." Pointing to the passenger, he said, "You wait quietly, you'll have your turn." Noah then nodded to the cab driver.

The man put the whip back in its holder, removed his top hat, and looked to Noah in a way meant to be both hurt and respectful. "My name is Stanley Alter and I'll tell it like it happened and dare any man to say different. I picked up my ride at Victoria Station. I ask him where he wants to go. He gives me the address of this place here and I say that's fine and we take off. We don't go five minutes when he says he needs to pick up or maybe it's drop off something, but anyway he tells me he needs to make a stop at his office, that it will just take a minute. That's what he says, 'that it will just take a minute.' So, I say fine, and I ask him for the address of his office. Which, it turns out is nowheres near to the route to his house. Besides which, it's more like fifteen or twenty minutes that I got to wait outside his office with at least two bobbies telling me to move on and me explaining I'm waiting on my fare. So, naturally with all that going on, I charge him two bob ten instead of the one bob ten it would have been for coming straight here with no stopping. And it's a good deal he's getting at that."

The passenger, who'd been groaning his dissatisfaction throughout the whole of the driver's characterization, could no longer contain himself. Although well into his fifties and slightly built, he appeared ready to challenge his younger, stockier opponent should Noah fail to see the merit of his position. "I am Michael Silver, and that man," pointing to the driver with as fierce a look as he could manage, "is either a liar or is entering his second childhood. My office is a street—at most two, off the route he would follow to get me home. And as for the brief stop at my office, in the first place I said, 'it should just take a few minutes.' I never said a minute. Nothing in life only takes a minute. And it did only take me maybe five minutes at most. And, instead of informing me of his intentions, it's only when we pull up to my house that he informs me he's added an extra shilling onto my fare, so rather than my owing one shilling, ten like it's always been, I owe two shillings, ten, which it never has been. The man's trying to rob me and I'd be happy to swear out a complaint or however it's done."

The driver now appeared ready to retrieve his whip from its holder, while his passenger was prepared to discount the formidable odds against him and abandon words for action. It was past time for Constable Lestrade to take control. He thought it best to begin by stating the absurdity of the situation.

"You gentlemen do understand you are arguing about a single shilling?"

It quickly became clear he had happened on a single point of agreement between the two men. Neither thought their argument absurd.

Silver spoke first, "It's not the money; it's the principle. A man can't suddenly change the rules to suit himself."

Alter then spoke his piece, "Well, first off, I'm not so rich that I can toss off shillings like they mean nothing to me. If I do it right, a shilling can buy me lunch. And the toff ain't the only one with principles. Like the one where you can't just do as you please and expect to get away with it."

The two glared at each other while each waited for the constable to rule in their favor. Such a ruling would please one man and gravely disappoint the other. Noah decided to gravely disappoint both.

"I know I'm dealing with two honorable men. You both claim to be acting on principle and I think that both of you are. I believe this to be an honest disagreement between two honorable men. Each of you believes he has right on his side and, understandably, wants the other to pay, or be paid, the fare that's right. It is, as I say, an honest disagreement. And there's no way now to know what was said about wait time and how the stop at the office changed the route home. All we can do is resolve the situation in the fairest way possible, which is to say in the way honorable gentlemen such as yourselves can do." Noah could see he was making progress of a sort, Alter and Silver were no longer glaring at each other, but were instead looking questioningly to him.

"What I'm now asking you to do, in the spirit of fairness, is to split the one shilling difference between you. Mr. Silver, you will pay an additional six pence to Mr. Alter, and Mr. Alter, you will forgo payment of the six pence beyond what you believe yourself to be owed."

As the two men grumbled their reservations about Noah's solution, the constable thought it wise to add one further note. "And that will make it unnecessary for me to take anyone to the station for disturbing the peace."

The grumbling seemed to reach a lower pitch and then disappear altogether coincident with Silver handing the suggested number of pence to Alter, and the coachman nodding acceptance of the payment. There was one last exchange before the two men parted company.

"There's no tip and I'm hoping never to see you in these parts again."

"Didn't expect no tip, and if I never see you again, I'll cry no tears about it."

Neither man said a word to Noah although each gave him a quick nod on leaving.

He got a far warmer greeting from Christabel, who had come away from where Noah had left her, and seen and heard enough of the exchange to revise somewhat her thinking about the constable.

"That was very well done, Constable Lestrade." To make clear the compliment, she inserted an arm in his as they continued their walk.

Whether from the compliment or its aftermath, he blushed slightly as he thanked her for her words. "It's nice of you to say so." In truth, Noah thought he had done rather well and was pleased there was a witness to his action. He was surprised to find himself particularly pleased to have Christabel Pankhurst as that witness.

They talked about police work and the movement for voting rights, but also about their families, their lives, and their plans for the future. When they returned to the Lestrade home, Christabel dropped to her side the arm she had linked to Noah's and Noah's smile was replaced by a look of businesslike detachment. Nonetheless, the eyebrows of two people briefly sought entry to their foreheads on observing the couple's entrance, one with some small unease and the other with some small amusement. Mrs. Lestrade made plans to speak to Detective Inspector Lestrade later that evening with the intent of sharing her small unease, while Annie Kenney planned to have a heart-to-heart talk with Christabel later that evening with the intent of increasing her small amusement.

Chapter 6.
Taking Stock of the Situation

With the table cleared of all but pencils and sheets of paper, Mrs. Hudson took her accustomed place at its head while Holmes and Watson sat to her right and left. They would rely on the careful notes she'd written after each meeting with the suspects, Holmes's jottings and the recollections of them both to review the progress thus far in the investigation. Mrs. Hudson thought their records would likely be adequate to the task, but knew she'd feel a great deal more confident if they had Dr. Watson's detailed reporting based on his well-practiced notetaking.

"Let us take stock of what we know about our suspects and consider what we still need to learn. We can consider them in the order they were interviewed. Dr. Watson, I'll ask you to take notes and to raise questions about whatever you find curious or unclear."

She punctuated her request with a quick nod to Watson, then began. "There's first off the Clarks, and the first of the two of them was Mrs. Clark. I think we can agree she 'ad good reason for wantin' to see no more of Reginald Miles. 'E uh … 'E first took advantage of 'er, which is 'ow I think the novels would put it, and then 'e came by pretty regularly, although unpredictably, askin' for 'er favors, and, when she refused, blackmailin' 'er by askin' for loans 'e never intended on payin' back as a price for 'is silence." She looked to the papers she had spread in front of her and nodded her satisfaction before adding a further point.

"So, 'ere was a woman who likely felt she 'ad good reason to want to see the last of Reginald Miles and, bein' the wife of an apothecary, she likely 'ad a way of doin' more than just *wantin'* to rid 'erself of Mr. Miles. And, like just about everybody else, Mrs. Clark spent some time out of the study when Dr. Watson was showin' 'is photographs where she could 'ave put poison in 'is wine glass. We know she left the study the same time as Mrs. Johnson and Mr. Clark, but they each came back separately meanin' she or any one of them, or two or more of them combined, had opportunity." Mrs. Hudson paused to take a second look at her notes. Finding nothing additional to report, she turned to Holmes. "Would you like to add anythin', Mr. 'Olmes?"

"Only that from your accounting, Mrs. Hudson, she was clearly deeply concerned with keeping her rendezvous with Miles secret from her husband and, if she thought Miles might approach him …. Let's just say she struck me as a very determined woman." Holmes looked to Watson, getting the deep, learned nod he was seeking, before settling back in his chair as Mrs. Hudson added a further observation.

"Of course, there could be some of the same issues for Mr. Clark as there are for Mrs. Clark—if Mr. Clark knew more about what was goin' on than 'e wanted to admit to us, which I believe to be the case. You remember, Mr. 'Olmes, when we asked 'im about Reginald Miles bein' a ladies' man, 'is face told us what 'is silence meant to keep secret. 'Is mouth got tight and 'e started blinkin' a whole lot, all of that tellin' us somethin' was gettin' stirred around in 'is 'ead that made 'im uncomfortable. And it was right after that 'e asked us to leave, as you'll remember."

Holmes remembered the question about Miles being a ladies' man and, now that he was reminded, thought he remembered a change in Miles's expression and their leaving the apothecary shop shortly thereafter. "I do believe that's right, Mrs. Hudson. And I, too, wondered about the families conspiring together, what with both having the same objective and facing the same impediments to their achieving those objectives."

Holmes turned to Watson for his assessment of the situation. "Watson, the Clarks were sitting near to you at dinner. Did they do or say anything that seemed to you unsettling?"

"I can't say they did, Holmes. I can only tell you that the Clarks didn't have much to say to Miles, but neither did anyone else except maybe Worthington. I can tell you they weren't the ones who started the negative talk about Miles and I don't believe they joined in. As I've said, after the talk got started, I believe it was his son, Edward, who suggested we take a break from the table before having dessert to sort of defuse the situation. Edward was also a help to me later on. He and Alice had seen the photographs earlier, when they came to visit not long after we got back from Scotland, so he could sort of fill in for me the one time I went to check on things in the kitchen. In fact, I believe they stayed close by the whole time to help out and probably never left the study." After a few seconds further searching his memory, Watson said he had nothing more to report about the Clarks and apologized for getting into a conversation about the younger Miles prematurely.

Mrs. Hudson rejected any need for concern on Watson's part, stating that she was about to recommend they move on to talk of what they knew about Edward and Alice Miles.

"While there's clearly no love lost by Edward for his father," Holmes observed, "any reason he would have for hurrying his father's death would seem related to the inheritance he would then receive assuming the unthinkable—that he could contrive a way to get you out of the picture as well, Watson. As we know Margaret's bequest to her sister and brother—and now her nephew—is likely to be sizable when it materializes. In a word, the portion that would pass to Edward Miles would be considerable enough to tempt a young man of large hopes and limited means."

"Or a woman," Watson added, "For the inheritance to reach Edward, there is needed ... I should say, was needed, the removal of both Reginald Miles and myself, assuming, of course, Miles made his only son his sole heir. For the inheritance to reach Violet, there is needed only the removal of me. In either event, or if, as we've suggested, people are working together, it doesn't say much for my longevity. If money is the motivation for murder, one impediment has been removed and a trip to the gallows will remove the other. If it's not too selfish, may I suggest we accelerate the effort to find Reginald Miles's real killer."

"Watson, you must know a trip to the gallows will never happen. We simply wouldn't allow it." Holmes assured his friend in the most strident tones he could muster.

"Of course not." Unable to match Holmes's fervor or precise diction, Mrs. Hudson vigorously shook her head several times as if to exorcise the thought before moving the conversation to what she thought would be a more productive, and certainly less depressing realm.

"It does appear to be the case, as Mr. 'Olmes 'as said, that both the Mileses and the Johnsons stand to gain a great deal from the kindness of Mrs. Watson. However, it seems as though the death of Reginald Miles only helps Edward and Alice Miles get closer to the money,

And while the Johnsons certainly 'ave strong feelin's about Mr. Miles, I'm not yet seein' where they've got a reason for murderin' the man. At the same time, Edward and Alice Miles, who do 'ave reason to want Reginald Miles dead, apparently never left the study which reduces, if it doesn't eliminate their opportunity to put the poison in Mr. Miles's glass. Besides all that, we'd 'ave to ask even with the money, and even with Reginald Miles bein' an awful father, can we see the son murderin' 'is own father?"

After a short pause to allow her comments their due consideration, Mrs. Hudson suggested they move on to a discussion of another of Watson's dinner guests.

"Let us then turn to Mr. Cyril Worthin'ton. 'E describes 'imself as a good friend of Mr. Miles back in earlier times, a friendship that seems to 'ave been based mostly on the interest they shared in gamblin'. It's an interest Mr. Worthin'ton says 'e never 'ad as bad as Mr. Miles and now 'as under control. Anyway, as a result of that and maybe some other things, Mr. Worthin'ton says the two men drifted apart."

"It's true, Mrs. Hudson, they were good friends, and they did drift apart. That's certainly what Margaret believed and what she told me. Margaret did tell me about Natalie suddenly breaking things off with Worthington and marrying Reginald. It was a decision she said she never understood. Margaret thought—or really hoped—it might lead Reginald to settle down, but, of course, it didn't. And we can assume all of that took a toll on Worthington and maybe still does. I'm sorry, I would have said something about it sooner, but in all the excitement I simply forgot. Anyway, it's exactly the kind of thing Margaret would have hoped could be resolved over a friendly dinner, what with all the time that's passed. I know it can be hard to see that, but Margaret was always more optimistic about resolving those kinds of problems than other people. Which, I suppose, explains her success in resolving them."

Watson smiled at a bittersweet memory others did not share even as they smiled at the hint of good feeling awakened in their colleague.

Holmes ended the brief period of silence that followed Watson's statement with a question that had concerned him from the outset of discussion about Worthington.

"The man is staying in a hotel. Does that affect the likelihood of his being our killer? I'm thinking particularly of his ability to acquire the cyanide that was used to poison Miles."

"One might think so, Holmes," Watson answered, "but the truth is cyanide is found in so many things, it would be easy for him to have obtained it somewhere else and brought it with him."

"There's somethin' else Mr. Worthin'ton talked about that will be important to keep in mind. Mr. Worthin'ton talked about Mr. Miles turnin' to loan sharks to take care of 'is wagerin'. I'm not sure 'ow that might enter into our investigation, but it definitely brings in a whole new concern. It was one thing when Mr. Miles was gettin' money from friends and acquaintances, whether it was real borrowin' or blackmail to look like borrowin'. Like Mr. Worthin'ton says, it's a lot different when you're borrowin' money from loan sharks. From everythin' I 'eard they don't wait patiently to be paid back. If Mr. Miles owed them money—and it certainly sounds like 'e did—'e would've been in a world of trouble with some very difficult people."

Neither Holmes nor Watson asked the source of her information about loan sharks or questioned its accuracy. They knew it came from Tobias Hudson and they knew there was no questioning the accuracy of the man she described as her "uncommon common constable."

Having given voice to all they considered of consequence about Cyril Worthington, attention turned to Wilson James, the last of the dinner guests to be considered. Holmes spoke first.

"The situation with James appears similar to what we've heard from Miles's other blackmail victims, with perhaps the not insignificant difference of Miles achieving a new low in his willingness to take advantage of the pathetic state of Mrs. James, and James's need to do whatever he could for his wife. I do think this is the most heinous example of the lengths to which Miles would go to obtain the money he needed to feed his compulsion."

"All that is true, but it doesn't make Mr. James any less of a suspect," Mrs. Hudson reminded her colleagues. "'E 'ad reason to want to rid 'imself of Mr. Miles since he still faced the prospect of blackmail whenever Mr. Miles decided 'e wanted to start that back up again. And I'm not forgettin' that Mr. Worthin'ton said 'e saw 'im leave the study, which I know makes 'im one of pretty near everybody, but it does give 'im opportunity, maybe like everybody else, but it's important to our consideration of 'im regardless. I'm thinkin' that it was Mr. James who maybe spoke the strongest about Mr. Miles. Even talkin' about shakin' the 'and of whoever poisoned 'im—which, of course, could also be 'is way of tryin' to throw us off 'is track."

"Are we back where we started, Mrs. Hudson? Everyone appears to have reason to want to see Miles dead and to have had the opportunity to make it happen, but the evidence—as far as the authorities are concerned—points to me." The plaintive question, coming from the always level-headed Watson, served to reawaken the sense of urgency Mrs. Hudson and Holmes felt for their friend and colleague.

It was left to Mrs. Hudson to find some note of hopefulness on which to end the meeting. She did her best in the face of a formidable task. "I'm thinkin' we've come up against tough problems before and we've come out alright. And we will see justice done 'ere as well, I promise that. For now, we'll need our sleep and see 'ow things look in the mornin'." Her expression of near confidence led to a near smile from Holmes, and a grunt of appreciation from Watson.

Chapter 7.
Swimming with Sharks

The truth was Mrs. Hudson was not as pessimistic as she sounded in her meeting with Holmes and Watson. There were hints, but just hints, of a solution to the puzzle of Reginald Miles's death that would exonerate Dr. Watson and identify the poisoner. Because they were just hints, and because her colleagues would be anxious to grab onto anything that smacked of the possibility of freeing Dr. Watson, she thought it wise to hold off sharing those hints at least until she felt certain they would blossom into full blown hunches.

She recognized that the evidence against Dr. Watson was all circumstantial but was nonetheless formidable. His very public statement months earlier holding Miles partially responsible for his wife's death could be seen as motivation, and opportunity was provided by his trip to the kitchen and the frosted glasses he had selected that would hide from plain view the cyanide put in one of them. Then, too, there was the continuing conflict between the two men with Miles charging Watson with marrying his sister for her money and implying, if not stating, that Watson had hurried along his gaining access to that money. Finally, and most dramatically, there was Miles's last word and gesture accusing Watson of his death. Mrs. Hudson had known juries to be convinced of a defendant's guilt with less certain evidence and judges to pass harsh sentences with equally flawed reasoning.

And so, her own fears about Watson's ultimate fate gnawed at Mrs. Hudson, allowing her only a fitful sleep. And still, she did better than her colleagues as Holmes and Watson lay sleepless, writhing their way through a succession of positions in hopes of finding one that would allow comfort. Thus, when the doorbell rang, it wakened only Mrs. Hudson although it instantly commanded the attention of all three Baker Street residents.

Each took the precautions deemed appropriate. Watson armed himself with his service revolver and, leaving the door of the lumber room slightly ajar, stood ready to take whatever action he believed to be needed. Holmes retrieved his Bartitsu stick and stood at the head of the stairs holding it overhead, his warrior image partially undone by the mauve dressing gown he wore over his nightshirt. Mrs. Hudson thought it unlikely that a thief or murderer would announce himself as noisily as whoever was on the other side of her front door. Nonetheless, she observed basic precautions, removing an umbrella from the stand by the door, and positioning it well above her head as she called out the obligatory questions.

"Who are you and what is it you want at this 'our?"

She waited fifteen seconds and, when there was still no response, she gave a nod to Holmes, then opened the door wide and stepped back quickly, umbrella still at the ready. At the same time, Holmes came halfway down the stairs, still brandishing the Bartitsu stick, now in one hand at shoulder level.

What they saw in the 221B doorway caused them to reassess the need for the weapons they carried. Ezra Perlmutter, as he introduced himself, was dressed for an evening out in far more elegant company than he could hope to find at 221B, even had his visit occurred at a more conventional hour. He wore a top hat, morning coat and striped trousers, and he dandled a cane clearly intended to complete the outfit of a gentleman rather than to provide support to his stride. He had a trim Vandyke beard that he scratched as he looked with amusement to his prospective host and hostess and the weapons they held. But neither his dress nor the face he made captured his audience's attention.

That was reserved for the size of the man—or rather his lack of size. He might have been a student in primary school playing at dress-up were it not for the disparaging look he now showed Holmes and Mrs. Hudson, making clear his modest stature was of no moment to Ezra Perlmutter and would be to others at their own risk.

He handed Mrs. Hudson his cane and top hat which she somewhat belatedly recognized she was expected to take from him. "I wonder if there's a place Mr. Holmes and I might talk."

"I believe the sittin' room will do nicely although it is in need of a good cleanin'." Mrs. Hudson had no idea why she felt constrained to make clear the state of the sitting room since she'd never done so before, even for visitors she knew to be high ranking officials, even for royals. In any event, and importantly, he would thereby be seated within hearing range of the lumber room.

"Excellent, if you would lead the way, Mr. Holmes, and might I trouble you for some tea, madam. Oh, and may I say I've heard only good things about your scones. If you happen to have any left, it would be much appreciated. Just let me signal to my colleague that I'll be a while." Opening the door, he waved to a man lounging beneath a lamppost across the roadway who waved back his understanding.

It was difficult for Mrs. Hudson and Holmes to decide which was the more impressive, his knowing enough of their business to be aware of Mrs. Hudson's scones or the burly figure across the roadway who easily made up in size what Ezra Perlmutter lacked.

Holmes climbed the seventeen steps to the sitting room followed by his mysterious visitor, while Mrs. Hudson readied a pot of tea in her kitchen and dug out what few scones remained from breakfast. Watson, meanwhile, stood silent at the barely open door to the lumber room, his revolver cocked and ready. When the two men had taken seats, Perlmutter smiled indulgently to his host and spoke words of apology that rang hollow with the speaker's thorough-going absence of contrition.

"I must ask your forgiveness for coming at this late hour. Nathan and I had some business to conduct before coming to visit you and I'm afraid it took somewhat longer than expected. You see, I work for an organization whose mission is to help people realize their dreams. The difficulty we run into is that sometimes people dream too big or on the wrong outcome. You wouldn't know about such things, Mr. Holmes, because you and the people I try to help have different dreams—not just in their nature, although in that too, but in their ability to cover their cost. Anyway, tonight Nathan and I had to meet with some people who accepted our help but whose dreams didn't work out. Now they owe us for the help we gave them, but they have a problem making payments. And that, of course, makes a problem for us. We visited them at this late hour to be sure we'd find them at home where we could clarify their problem and help them work out a plan to rid themselves of that problem.

"I'm sure you notice I say 'we' as I talk about things. That's not just about my friend across the roadway. The two of us work for some very important, very powerful people. They're also very private people so we don't bandy their names around. Still, you should keep in mind that there are these people.

"Ah, but here is our tea and scones." He gave Mrs. Hudson a broad smile which appeared to her as genuine as his earlier apology for his late arrival. "Maybe we can save one for my colleague outside when we're done. We'll keep him outside for now. I don't believe he's needed for this meeting."

With that, he took a scone from Mrs. Hudson's tray, took a bite that was well beyond exploratory, and shut his eyes for the moment as he savored his prize. He dabbed his mouth with the napkin Mrs. Hudson had also provided before pronouncing what his actions had already made clear.

"Your reputation is clearly well earned, Mrs. Hudson. These are the finest baked goods I've had since I truly don't know when. Perhaps the next time I come you can bake enough for me to take some back with me. I would, of course, be happy to pay any amount you deem fair."

Having learned nothing about his unwelcome guest beyond a fondness for scones and his seemingly considerable knowledge of life at 221B, Holmes decided it was well past time for him to take a measure of control over events in a home he had come to regard as his own. Ignoring the tray of scones—which Mrs. Hudson recognized as a sure sign of his annoyance—and adopting a stentorian tone, he sought to bring their small menace to heel.

"You have arrived at our home in the middle of the night for reasons I can't imagine and requested a level of hospitality to which you clearly feel entitled and to which I feel you are clearly not entitled. Now, I'm asking you to state your business and leave, or simply to leave. It makes no difference to me which. And I'm sure I speak for Mrs. Hudson in this regard." Mrs. Hudson nodded support for her colleague.

The recipient of the invitation to leave smiled softly and took a second bite of his scone. "I understand that the hour causes us all to be a little testy. Perhaps when you hear my proposal you'll feel better about my visit. The fact is I have something to offer that I believe can greatly benefit the both of us. I do, of course, have the capacity to achieve my objectives working solely with my own people, but I felt a certain respect was due the renowned Sherlock Holmes. Besides which, I must admit I would feel it a feather in my cap to say I joined forces with Sherlock Holmes—even if only briefly. But let me now put to you the plan I have in mind, and you can tell me of your interest. I assume Mrs.

Hudson is sufficiently involved in your work that she needn't be required to leave if she cares to stay. In any event, she already knows of my arrival here and so must be regarded as a participant in any future action. In that regard, I'm obliged to warn the both of you that whatever we discuss is to go no further than this room. It would be a very unhappy situation if things went otherwise.

"For now, no one knows I'm here. I'm to work things out with you and only after we talk will my people be given the details of our agreement. That way if anything goes wrong, they're not involved. Tomorrow, or I guess later today, after things are sorted, I'll tell them of our little discussion, and, I trust, I'll be able to share our agreement."

He looked to his audience to confirm that he had, as expected, their rapt attention as well as their silence. Armed with those two essentials, he set forth his proposal.

"I know you are working very hard to get your friend, Dr. Watson, free of his murder charge and that you're having problems getting that worked out." Looking to two pairs of raised eyebrows, Perlmutter waved away the question they reflected. "It doesn't matter how I know these things. Just keep in mind the people I work for make it their business to know such things, and already know things about you, you may not know yourself."

Perlmutter retrieved a second scone from the tray and bit off a corner which he chewed thoroughly before resuming his speech. "As I was saying, you're having trouble proving your friend's innocence. You want him cleared and I want—which means my people want—the money Miles owes us." A second bite and its thorough mastication preceded further speech.

"I have a way for us both to get what we want. The people I represent will see to it that the charges against Dr. Watson are dropped in exchange for his sharing with us the money owed us by Reginald Miles. The money would come

114

from the inheritance left him by his wife, so you see in a way it's found money he wasn't expecting and won't miss. I should make clear we are not avaricious people. We only want what Mr. Miles owes us, no more and no less. I can, of course, produce the betting slips and markers if you wish to confirm what we know to be the money owed us, but I'm hoping we're at a level of trust that makes such action unnecessary." A third bite of his scone seemed to remind Perlmutter of something he had not yet shared.

"Of course, your Watson need not hand over what we are owed in one lump sum. We will work out a payment schedule with dates and amounts due. I'm sure you can appreciate the importance of making timely payments and will not make the same mistake in that regard that was made by Mr. Miles." The last of the scone now disappeared into Perlmutter's mouth.

Holmes slowly and purposefully crossed the floor as Perlmutter spoke, retrieved his briar from the mantle and began to fill it with the black shag he favored. Mrs. Hudson gave silent approval to his show of unconcern and waited the questioning she knew would be forthcoming.

"You say you—or your people—can get the charges against Dr. Watson dropped, but you've said nothing about how you—or your people—would get that done." The tobacco tamped down, Holmes now lit his pipe and watched a small cloud of smoke waft its way slowly to the sitting room ceiling.

Perlmutter smiled his appreciation of their small duel. "I would suggest you not concern yourself with those details. Trust me, it will be done."

"I'm sure you and your people enjoy a fine reputation for doing whatever it is you do, but I have never worked with you or your people and there's more I need to know, specifically how do you propose to establish Dr. Watson's innocence."

Perlmutter steepled his fingers to his mouth, shrugged, then dropped his hands to his lap as he spoke to Holmes's concern. "Several strategies would be available. It's not really my area, but I suppose the cleanest, neatest strategy would be to establish someone else's guilt."

"You mean you can identify the person who killed Reginald Miles?"

"This is why I suggested you not concern yourself with details. What I'm saying is that we can establish someone else's guilt. There may be other solutions available. As I've said, it's not my particular area of operations. The important thing is, that whatever strategy is chosen, it will allow your friend to go free, and if you reject the strategy, your friend will almost certainly hang. I don't see that there's much choice, but seeing that it's you, Mr. Holmes, I'll give you the rest of the day to think about it. I'll be in touch after dark, although not as late as tonight. I will report to my people that we didn't conclude our business due to the lateness of the hour, but I fully expect to reach a mutually satisfactory agreement when we meet next time. You should understand my people would expect me to have things wrapped up by now. They're not patient people, Mr. Holmes."

Only as Ezra Perlmutter got to his feet, scooped up the scone for his colleague and walked to the stairs, did Mrs. Hudson and Holmes again become aware of the size of the man offering to trade Watson's life for an unspecified other. There was no sharing of good-byes as he opened the front door and exited to Baker Street, signaling his colleague across the roadway to join him in the waiting hansom.

Watson came to where they stood at the head of the stairs to marvel with his colleagues at the scene just ended. They agreed they would each consider what they had witnessed in their own rooms and beds and discuss it after the sun was up, in the unlikely event any of them slept some part of the remaining night.

Sun-up brought no relief from the evening's gloom. Neither Mrs. Hudson's breakfast, including the kippers and sausage both men favored, nor even the fresh baked scones Mrs. Hudson had managed, "as long as I was up anyway," could dispel from awareness the image of the diminutive Ezra Perlmutter, his burly confederate, or their unseen but well imagined "people." Each man made a spirited attempt to deal with the plates set before him, if only to please Mrs. Hudson. but it became quickly apparent they were incapable of making a respectable assault on the breakfast dishes.

They had all but decided to limit the morning's breakfast to a few pieces of toast and tea and move right into a discussion of how to respond to the nighttime visit of Ezra Perlmutter when the doorbell rang interrupting those plans.

They were momentarily relieved to find Lucinda Wiggins at their door, the relief lasting only until they caught sight of an uncharacteristic tension in her manner.

At Mrs. Hudson's invitation, she joined them at the table, initially rejecting the offer of breakfast, and only agreeing to reconsider after Mrs. Hudson had assured her that there was more food than they could possibly eat, and she would be doing them a favor by eating at least some of what they would otherwise be forced to throw away. She agreed but only after justifying her decision with the explanation she had come to see them at Tommy's insistence, without stopping for breakfast.

Speaking between hurried bites, Lucinda shared the message she and Tommy had agreed to be urgent. "We both thought you should know there is another march for women's votes planned for Sunday, just two days from now. Tommy thought, and I agree, that when Miss Pankhurst and Miss Kenney hear about it, they'll plan to go regardless of their

117

being on house arrest and, as a result, there'll just be more trouble for everyone. Tommy and me didn't know what could be done about it, but we thought you would want to know." Having delivered her message, Lucinda concentrated her attention on the two kippers she had pulled from the serving plate.

While Holmes maintained a look of glum concentration that Lucinda took to be a sign of his carefully weighing the several options that had come to mind, Mrs. Hudson sought to confirm her suspicions about Lucinda's plans for the morning. She decided a direct approach would yield the most information.

"Will you be seein' Miss Pankhurst and Miss Kenney while you're out?"

The faintest blush started to capture Lucinda's cheeks. "I was thinking of visiting Mr. and Mrs. Lestrade and seeing Millicent and Miss Pankhurst and Miss Kenney just to make sure that everything's alright and to find out if there's anything I can do." The last part of one kipper disappeared into Lucinda's mouth, for the moment cutting off any further elaboration of her plans. Mrs. Hudson guessed at them with what she was certain was great accuracy.

"I'm thinkin' that with you now bein' a friend of Millicent's and the two ladies, it would be only natural for you to want to find out what exactly everyone knows about the march, and maybe 'ow the two ladies are plannin' to get to the march, and just maybe what you can do to 'elp."

The blush that had earlier begun to invade Lucinda's cheeks now took them over completely as Lucinda recognized that the small deception she had painstakingly put together had come completely undone. She was saved further embarrassment by the small deception Mrs. Hudson put forward.

"You should know Mr. 'Olmes 'as got 'is own plans for the day. There's still the rock-throwers to catch to get

Miss Pankhurst and Miss Kenney permanently free of any charges. It's maybe oversteppin' my bounds, Mr. 'Olmes," she gave her colleague as close to a confidential look as she could muster, "but I know your ways and 'ow you like to keep things to yourself until your own good time for sharin'. Until then, it will be wise to take no action that might conflict with Mr. 'Olmes's plans." Mrs. Hudson now looked to Lucinda with a stare meant to be withering to carry home her concern that no action should be taken until Mr. Holmes had access to the plan she was yet to divulge to him.

Feeling he should lay claim to ownership of that plan whatever it was, Holmes addressed his landlady in a tone appropriate to addressing a housekeeper. "Quite right, Mrs. Hudson, but I do wish that in the future you'd keep to yourself any planning you happen to overhear."

Having delivered her news, and anxious to escape whatever small domestic disturbance might be brewing, Lucinda spoke of the need to be on her way, promising to say nothing about Mr. Holmes's plan, of which she conveniently knew nothing. Even as Lucinda was closing the door behind her, dishes other than teacups were being removed from the breakfast table, scraped, and placed in Mrs. Hudson's tub. They were replaced by a pot of tea, lemon, and milk, cups and saucers, and the writing paper and Number 2 Eagle pencil Watson had retrieved from his desk. Taking their usual seats with Mrs. Hudson at the head of the table, and Holmes and Watson to her right and left, Mrs. Hudson set the agenda for their meeting.

"We need to discuss our response to Mr. Perlmutter and then work out what we want to do about the march Lucinda spoke about. I'm thinkin' the march gives us a good chance to catch the real rock-throwers and let Miss Pankhurst and Miss Kenney get on with their lives. It seems to me likely our rock-throwers will be out again at this march with an eye to gettin' some other of the suffragettes in trouble with the law. We've got a little bit of time on that one and I've got some thoughts, so we'll put it aside for the moment while we talk about Mr. Perlmutter." She poured a cup of tea for herself and found no other takers as Holmes and Watson were both anxious to hear her thinking about Perlmutter.

"I believe that we're all in agreement as to the appropriate response to Mr. Perlmutter's proposal." As expected, she got two vigorous nods.

"Mr. 'Olmes, I'm askin' you to deliver that message when Mr. Perlmutter gets 'ere. 'E won't be 'appy about it, seein' as 'ow 'e thinks 'is offer is one for which we should be thankful. Still, I don't see there bein' a problem for us, at least not right off. Just to be safe, I'll ask Constable Chase to keep an eye on things. That won't be the end of it, of course. We know they won't stop at anythin' to get the money they say Mr. Miles owed them. We can guess that when they finish with us, their next move could be to visit with Edward Miles and 'is wife to work somethin' out with them. We 'ave to be ready for that somethin' bein' their willin'ness to strengthen the case against Dr. Watson in exchange for the Miles's promise to sign over as much of the inheritance as needed to pay off Mr. Miles's debt."

She paused to carefully add a note of optimism into the dismal analysis. The situation called for more than a note, but her idea was just as outlandish today as it had been the day before when she kept it to herself and so a note would have to do. And there was justification for expressing some degree of optimism on two counts. On the one hand, the mood had turned so dark, she felt obliged to give her colleagues some reason for hope. On the other, she had come to a place in her own thinking where, having eliminated all else, the improbable that remained seemed likely to be the truth. "I'm thinkin' I see where there could be a way out of this but it's just a 'unch for now and still needs work."

Both men brightened instantly. They had been frequent witnesses to Mrs. Hudson's hunches and had always seen them blossom into full-blown solutions. And still, Watson felt obliged to share his latest fear born of the meeting with Perlmutter.

"There's another possibility, Mrs. Hudson. Mr. Perlmutter, or his people, could decide that if the person who stands accused of murder is found dead, and the death is made to look like a suicide, it might hurry along the disbursal of the inheritance to Margaret's sister and nephew, and thereby get it a step closer to Perlmutter and whoever he represents. Besides which, it would close the book on Reginald Miles's murder with me seen as having committed suicide because of the guilt I felt for poisoning him."

Holmes was determined to dispel any thought of failure in their investigation, and most especially any thought of Watson suffering the unthinkable. "We will be constantly on guard against anything like that happening, Watson. Still, if it will give you peace of mind, you might want to keep your service revolver handy."

Mrs. Hudson gave a quick nod to Holmes's comment before moving the conversation to the second topic she meant to cover.

"Dr. Watson remains, of course, our first concern, but we owe it to Inspector Lestrade and his family, as well of course to Miss Pankhurst and Miss Kenney, to make use of the upcomin' march to do somethin' about their problem. We did, after all, involve the Lestrades in our effort to protect the ladies." While no one spoke to it, all recognized that it was Mrs. Hudson who got the Lestrades involved with the effort to protect the ladies.

An hour later, after a number of questions from Holmes and Watson, and with Holmes's reservations addressed if not wholly resolved, a plan was adopted if only because of its being the best of the few bad options available.

With that done, and with all three still groggy from the last night's visitation, Mrs. Hudson declared it a day to be spent at rest—at least until Ezra Perlmutter arrived. She suggested Mr. Holmes review for himself how he wanted to express his refusal of Perlmutter's proposition, encouraging him to be dismissive without becoming too unpleasant, a certain amount of unpleasantness, however, being clearly warranted in her judgment.

While Holmes prepared himself for Perlmutter, Mrs. Hudson did her own preparation—that of scones as a reward for Mr. Holmes after what promised to be an unpleasant meeting was concluded, and for Dr. Watson in hopes of buoying his spirits at least a little.

Watson, in fact, had great confidence in his colleagues' ability to see justice prevail—at least up to now—and therefore determined to close his mind to any but positive outcomes and so turned his attention as best he could to the most recent issue of *Lancet* that had gone unread in the wake of his murder inquiry. He turned to Bevan's "Mistakes in the diagnosis of infectious disease," which he felt he should read for the sake of his practice, in the event he would one day be able to resume his practice. However, it soon developed that, instead of becoming engaged in Dr. Bevan's learned account, he found himself seeing again Reginald Miles supporting himself with one hand on the dining room table and with the other pointing to him before falling limp across the table.

The ringing of the doorbell interrupted Watson's melancholy daydreaming as well as all other activities at 221B. The sun was still well above the horizon, making it unlikely that Perlmutter had returned. Nonetheless, by tacit agreement all three resumed their defensive positions. Watson again retreated to the lumber room, again pocketing his service revolver as he left the door just enough ajar for him to make out most of the conversation from the sitting room. Holmes waited at the top of the stairs, no Bartitsu stick but with hands at the ready. With both men properly stationed, Mrs. Hudson opened the door wide and looking to where she would be face to face with Ezra Perlmutter, she found herself facing the impressive upper torso of the man she recognized as Perlmutter's sturdy companion from across the roadway.

Unlike his companion of the night before, he waited on the doorstep until invited to enter. Nonetheless, whatever the restraints he placed on himself, a confident smile made clear his expectation that an invitation would be issued shortly.

"Ezra will not be coming. My name is Nathan. I need to speak to your Mr. Holmes. "

Mrs. Hudson nodded the understanding she did not yet have and opened the door wide as a welcome to Ezra's burly replacement. Holmes had heard enough of the conversation to understand that things were about to go somewhat differently than he expected. How differently and why there would be a difference was yet to be discovered. He joined Mrs. Hudson and Nathan in the entry hall, explaining that he was Sherlock Holmes and that they could talk in the sitting room upstairs. He then invited Mrs. Hudson to bring them tea and scones and started for the stairs, only to find himself leading without a following, a situation the still smiling Nathan sought to correct.

"You're to come with me."

"Why would I do that? Where do you wish to take me? Where is Mr. Perlmutter?"

"You'll see. You'll see everything after you come with me."

Holmes was perplexed. So much so, that he looked to Mrs. Hudson for guidance but received only a headshake and raised eyebrows. With Constable Chase nowhere in sight, and obstinacy an ineffective weapon against a foe with unknown resources, he decided, finally, to accompany Nathan on whatever journey he had in mind. He did, however, take the precaution of removing his cane from the stand by the door, and flourishing it dramatically for Nathan's benefit before letting it come to rest by his side.

They proceeded to the carriage Nathan had waiting. Holmes listened for the address to which they'd be going and memorized it, although he thought it might only be of interest to his undertaker. Nathan pointed to the sun streaming in the cab and leaned across Holmes to pull down the curtain at his window, then straightened to pull down the curtain at his own window, all without losing the smile that seemed to Holmes a permanent fixture.

Holmes decided to attempt conversation with the cordial sphinx beside him although he felt it to be almost certainly pointless. "I wonder how long we can count on this good weather continuing."

Nathan stared silently ahead, still with his soft smile, but showing no sign of having even heard Holmes.

Holmes decided to take a somewhat more controversial position, while still dealing with the same inoffensive subject, and to ask for his companion's opinion. "I believe we're in for a harsh winter judging by the fall weather. What do you think, Nathan?"

Again, there was no sign that Holmes had been heard. And still there remained the smile, no longer taken as a sign of geniality, now suggesting to Holmes the menace he should have seen from the start.

Holmes gave up his short-lived efforts at sociability and sat the next twenty minutes in silence until Nathan became nearly verbose as the coach slowed to a stop.

"We're here."

Holmes half expected a blindfold as he exited the coach. Indeed, he hoped he would be given a blindfold. A blindfold would signal the need to keep him ignorant of his surroundings, which would mean he could expect to be returned to 221B when whatever awaited him was done.

In spite of his foreboding, Holmes couldn't help being impressed by the uniqueness of the house to which he was being guided by Nathan. He'd certainly seen larger and some grander houses, but none with the features of this one. Its owner, not content with the usual single turret to one side of the main residence, had purchased or perhaps commissioned a home with two broad turrets to either side of the multi-windowed main residence topped by a gambrel roof, its two sloping sides framed by the turrets. They crossed a long well-manicured lawn of a size commensurate with the size of the house, went up the few steps to a broad porch with widely spaced narrow columns seemingly in support of the floor above.

Nathan seized the ring in the mouth of a displeased appearing lion and rapped twice on the door. Rather than being greeted by the expected housekeeper, the door was opened by a tall, slender man in shirtsleeves, the man already balding although Holmes would describe him as in his mid-thirties at most.

The balding man gave a curt nod to Nathan, and an even curter nod to Holmes, before entering into the spirited conversation to which Holmes was becoming accustomed.

"Wait here." He then left them to mount the broad staircase and, Holmes presumed, to announce his arrival to whatever forces awaited him.

As it turned out, Holmes did not have long to wait to be introduced to those forces. The balding man reappeared on the stairs, stopped several steps from the bottom and issued his directive. "This way." He then turned to remount the stairs, never feeling the need to look back to be certain Holmes was following him.

As Holmes joined the balding man on the stairs, Nathan, who had waited with him until now, grunted a kind of farewell before disappearing through a door beyond the stairs, still showing the same enigmatic smile.

Holmes followed the balding man up the one flight of stairs, then down a corridor nearly to its end. The balding man knocked on the door of the room at which he stopped, heard the word "Enter," and, throwing the door open, motioned for Holmes to go through. His work done, the balding man retraced his steps back up the corridor, leaving Holmes to learn what fate was in store for him.

The room Holmes entered seemed cavernous, its considerable size accentuated by its near total lack of furnishings. There was a file cabinet in one corner, and a desk and swivel chair centered at the far wall, facing the door he had entered. Beyond that, there was only a single wooden chair set at the desk opposite the swivel chair. Holmes's choice was clear. He could stand or take the single seat available. He accepted the invitation to sit implied by the extended hand of the man occupying the swivel chair. Apparently feeling the need for some more substantial greeting, the man rose from his chair in what seemed a not inconsiderable feat. While the man was of moderate height, his horizontal dimensions were extraordinary.

Keeping two fists on the desk in support of his bulk, he issued more words to Holmes than he had heard in the last half-hour. "Good morning, Mr. Holmes. My name is Garfoyle. Everett Garfoyle. We've never met, but you may recall meeting my uncle, Gregory Garfoyle. Not, I have to say under the most auspicious of circumstances, but one can't always choose the circumstances that bring people together. But look at me, I'm being a terrible host. Can I get you some tea?" Holmes shook off the suggestion. "Coffee?" Another headshake. "Perhaps crumpets? They're fresh baked and delicious. Much more of a treat than scones, whose appeal I could never understand." This time Holmes nodded acceptance.

Holmes did, indeed, remember Gregory Garfoyle and, with that memory stirred, was feeling much more certain of returning to Baker Street later in the day. He had known him simply as Garfoyle, having been introduced under the trying circumstances to which his host referred. In any event, he now recognized a clear family resemblance in the three chins each Garfoyle possessed and their body dimensions more generally.

Garfoyle shouted his order for crumpets to the open door, obviously confident from prior experience it would be heard and obeyed. The giving of orders and confidence in their being carried out again put Holmes in mind of Gregory Garfoyle. It had been in the course of investigating the death of a boxer, Sailor Mackenzie, that he came in contact with Everett Garfoyle's uncle. It was then he discovered that Everett Garfoyle's grandfather had likely encouraged a murder and that his uncle was almost certainly involved in arranging the outcomes of boxing matches well before the fighters stepped into the ring. As it had turned out, the events involving the grandfather were lost in time, key witnesses having long since passed away and the senior Garfoyle well into his second childhood. The evidence for the fixing of boxing matches proved similarly elusive. Moreover, the practice itself was no novelty and would, according to Lestrade, who had also come on the scene, be deemed not worth prosecuting, making an arrest pointless. However happenstance the events, Holmes understood that Garfoyle was grateful for the intercession he believed Holmes had made.

"I like to think, Mr. Holmes, that I don't forget a favor. You did something for my uncle and grandfather, and, in that sense, you did something for me, and I owe you for that. Really, because two members of my family were involved at two different times, I owe you double."

A small look of confusion appeared, then disappeared from Holmes's face. It stayed long enough to be seen by Garfoyle and he responded to it. "Without your help, Mr. Holmes, we would almost certainly have been put out of our family business, if not by the authorities, then by another family in the same line of work. I assure you, Mr. Holmes, ours is a very competitive business. Families are always emerging who believe they can do your family's work better. But that's another topic."

Garfoyle noisily cleared his throat signaling his dismissal of any further discussion of the family business. "But that's all history and of no further concern. Now, I am prepared to do something for you to pay my debt. For starters, you will never see Ezra Perlmutter again. Perlmutter is a good man, but maybe just a little too independent at times. As I'm sure you've guessed, making things uncomfortable for you and your household was his idea and hadn't been approved by me. It can be, I admit, something we do but not to Sherlock Holmes. I'll let Ezra cool his heels for a while and I'm sure he'll do just fine the next time he's needed.

"Still, a part of what he proposed could make good sense. You want your friend—this Watson—to be seen as innocent of killing Miles, we want to get the money Miles owes us. Perlmutter's idea about finding someone else to take the blame—we'll handle that—and your Watson reimbursing us what Miles owed, does allow everyone to get what they want."

"Except for the person chosen to be found a murderer."

Everett Garfoyole softly snickered at Holmes's concern. "I assure you, Mr. Holmes, we will choose that person wisely. Indeed, you can participate in making the choice if you like." He stopped to look meaningfully to Holmes. "That's not an offer I've ever made before."

He interrupted himself long enough to acknowledge the tea and crumpets set on a corner of his desk by a young woman who backed from the room without acknowledging, or being acknowledged, by the men she served.

"I took the liberty of ordering tea in case you changed your mind, and I want your opinion of the crumpets before we go any further. Are they not a particular treat, not terribly crusty like your typical scone." Garfoyle waited Holmes's assessment with eyes widened.

Holmes did not feel this was a fight worth making. He bit off a good-sized bit of crumpet and pronounced it the finest crumpet he'd had in ages. Ages being the actual last time he'd had crumpets. Garfoyle's eyes resumed their normal size, and he smiled broadly, while it went unnoticed that Holmes did not take another bite.

With the test of his gourmet skills successfully concluded, Holmes felt himself returned to suddenly shaky ground. He'd been presented a proposal that the man who could be his captor regarded as generous, indeed as unprecedented in its generosity. He unexpectedly found himself wondering how his landlady would respond, and, even more surprisingly, believed he knew. Armed with that knowledge, he made his response.

"You must understand, Mr. Garfoyle, that tempting as your offer is, it simply wouldn't work because the idea of a substitute victim for Watson is not just known to me but was also heard by Mrs. … my landlady and she will answer truthfully any question put to her." Holmes then added an element that Mrs. Hudson would not have spoken. "The poor woman lacks the imagination to dissemble."

Garfoyle drew in a long breath and exhaled a bit longer. He then steepled stubby fingers to his chin preliminary to addressing the problem Holmes had created for him.

"Mr. Holmes, as I've said, my family is indebted to you, which means I am indebted to you—but only up to a point. And so, even as I'd like to be helpful, business is business and if I can't arrange—we can't arrange—to have someone else take the fall, I will have to ensure that your Dr. Watson does. And you know I can do that."

Holmes nodded his agreement with Garfoyle's estimate of his powers, then set forth his own proposal. It contained risk, possibly significant risk, and went beyond what had been discussed with Mrs. Hudson. Nonetheless, he saw no solution that didn't involve risk—significant risk—and he had to move Garfoyle away from sacrificing anyone he felt stood in the way of his getting the money he felt himself due. Success would ultimately depend on the accuracy of Mrs. Hudson's hunch, but he had never known any of her hunches to fail.

"You're a sporting man, Mr. Garfoyle. I have a sporting proposition for you. If I can't prove Watson's innocence in one week, I will pay you twice whatever it is Reginald Miles owes you, but if I do prove him to be innocent, you will abandon all thoughts of making him appear the guilty party or of implicating any innocent person in Miles's death."

Garfoyle smiled in a way that put Holmes in mind of cats and canaries. "How do you know you can trust me or that I can trust you?"

"I take it that you are a gentleman and the establishment of guarantees of good faith is unnecessary. Still, since you raise the issue, I suggest we both affix our names to a statement affirming the agreed-on terms of our wager, making a copy of that document available to each of us, and thereby allowing for a common understanding of our obligations to each other."

Garfoyle swallowed the snicker he'd begun. "Should you ever wish to cross to my side of the law, you should contact me." With that, Garfoyle swiveled his way to show Holmes his back as he lapsed into a brief silence to consider Holmes's proposal. When he turned back, he pulled himself as close as he was able to a bolt upright sitting position and clapped his hands. "Consider it done except, I will give you ten days rather than a week and allow you to write the agreement. That's how much of a gentleman I am and how much of a gentleman I take you to be." Nonetheless, before finalizing their agreement, the two gentlemen agreed that each would have two copies of the agreement, one for themselves, and one for someone they trusted, whose name would only be known to the signatory with whom he was associated.

The negotiations concluded, Garfoyle summoned the bald-headed man to furnish Holmes with paper, and pen and ink, and to place him in the adjoining room which turned out to be no better furnished than Garfoyle's office but had the decorating advantage of being far smaller and thereby less obviously bereft of furnishings. When Holmes had finished writing out the statement he believed they had agreed to, he checked the document with Garfoyle who made two changes that were so minor Holmes was convinced they were only made to make clear Garfoyle's continuing control of the situation. With two copies for each of them made available, Garfoyle directed the bald-headed man to hail a hansom for Holmes to allow his return to Baker Street. When he was again alone with Holmes, he had some parting words that left Holmes bewildered as to how to respond.

"You are aware, Mr. Holmes, that my actions on behalf of your Dr. Watson satisfy only one of my debts to you. There is still a second that I insist on discharging. However, the hour is late and we do not have to agree now on what that something will be, but you should keep this conversation in mind. I will be sending for you sometime soon. Perhaps with Mr. Perlmutter." With that, laughter began somewhere deep in the bowels of Garfoyle's body and only slowly made its way up to his mouth, jowls and chins shaking in its path. When he had achieved a measure of control, Garfoyle continued, "but I'm sure it won't come to that. Good day, Mr. Holmes. It's been good doing business with you." He gave Holmes a small wave but made no effort to rise to the occasion.

In the quiet of the hansom cab, Holmes considered his actions over the last hour and pronounced them well done. He felt certain his colleagues would agree. Negotiations had led to a seemingly small window of availability for establishing Watson's innocence, even with Garfoyle having widened it some, but the fact was that ten days was well within the timeframe needed to solve other cases and this one had the advantage of Mrs. Hudson's hunch. There was the matter of the second debt to be paid but Holmes thought they would have long since completed business with Garfoyle before the need arose to erase whatever debt the would-be benefactor had in mind.

His arrival at 221B was treated as cause for a holiday. Relief was written on the faces of both his colleagues, and his recitation of the encounter with Garfoyle was heard with wide-eyed admiration as well as a fresh pot of tea and a plateful of newly baked scones. He described Garfoyle's beliefs about the debts he owed but felt it unnecessary to report every detail of their encounter, and left out Garfoyle's role in extending the time for establishing Watson's innocence as well as any hint of the wager he had entered into. All in all, Holmes's only regret was the compliment he had paid Garfoyle's crumpets.

With the events of a busy and stressful day behind them, Holmes and Watson were ready to take comfort in a shared pipeful, perhaps two, but Mrs. Hudson reminded them of their commitment to exonerating Miss Pankhurst and Miss

Kenney, and returning the Lestrade home once again to the Lestrades alone. Having said that, she also had to acknowledge Holmes's point that neither Mrs. Lestrade or Millicent appeared to feel any urgency about the two women leaving their home. She said nothing further on that score but was aware from what she was hearing that Noah also seemed increasingly of two minds about at least one of the women's leaving. Nonetheless, they owed it to the inspector, she insisted, to remove any risk of his being seen as harboring fugitives in his home, and to the women to remove the stigma associated with their being fugitives.

At length, it was agreed that Mrs. Hudson would, in Holmes's name, make the telephone calls needed to set the stage for the ultimate exoneration of Miss Pankhurst and Miss Kenney, while Holmes and Watson took a one pipeful break from their labors and made a much delayed visit to the sitting room to engage in conversation on several subjects and a number of people—none of them named Nathan or Garfoyle or Ezra Perlmutter.

The telephone calls were completed quickly, and arrangements made to meet at the Lestrades in the late morning of the next day. It left Mrs. Hudson with one more task to complete before her workday was done. Dinner would shortly occupy the attention of her two colleagues. Whatever their wishes, she had neither the time nor the energy for anything elaborate and so began preparation of a simple vegetable soup, to be followed by fried sole, roasted potatoes and braised carrots. Any grousing about the rest of the meal would, she was certain, be mitigated by their positive feelings for its finish—bread and butter pudding which, in their judgment, ranked second only to scones in Mrs. Hudson's repertoire.

Chapter 8.
The Women's March for Votes

At eleven o'clock the next morning, Holmes, and Thomas and Lucinda Wiggins joined the two suffragettes and the entire Lestrade family in a dining room designed to accommodate six comfortably, eight with difficulty, and the nine now assembled not at all. Holmes elected to remain standing in spite of the earnest protestations of Mrs. Lestrade and the more subdued entreaties of the inspector. Both claimed a chair could be brought in from the den and space found. In fact, it suited Holmes to stand, allowing him to be seen as the group's leader as he began his presentation.

"As you know, we are here to decide on a course of action that will establish the innocence of Misses Pankhurst and Kenney. I am proposing, in that regard, that we use tomorrow's march to learn the identity of the rock-throwers. It seems to me likely that those intent on tarnishing the reputation of the women taking part in these demonstrations will use tomorrow's march to strike again."

"You do understand, Mr. Holmes, it isn't just women participating; there are right-thinking men who have the courage to join us." Christabel Pankhurst's comment spoke to all who were present, but her eyes seemed to search out one attendee in particular.

"As you say, Miss Pankhurst. Indeed, I am proposing that men be very much involved in the action I have in mind." He paused for the moment, assuring, if assurance was needed, that his audience would hang on his every word.

"Miss Pankhurst, Miss Kenney, you will need to be at the march tomorrow to identify the rock-throwers. You will, of course, be disguised, lest the rock-throwers recognize you and modify their behavior, or a sharp-eyed member of the constabulary makes you out and interferes with our plans. You are, of course, still subject to the demands of house arrest. However, while we mean to observe the spirit of those demands, it will be necessary to deviate some from the letter of those demands."

"In a word, you mean to break the law."

It was an objection for which the prior evening's practice had prepared Holmes.

"Constable Lestrade, as you are aware, the authorities have already broadened the definition of house arrest to include homes such as yours having the capacity to provide on-going surveillance. Indeed, I have heard of instances in which those accused of breaking the law have gone for walks on London's streets—under supervision, of course." He gave the constable the best part of a crooked smile and the constable glared at him in return. Regardless, Holmes was emboldened to continue.

"I mean for us to do little more in that regard than has already been done and I promise the ladies will remain under observation the entire time." For the moment, Holmes thought it wise to keep silent the details of how that observation would be conducted.

"May I assume you ladies still have the costumes that made you appear significantly ... larger than you really are?" His question was met with two less than enthusiastic nods. Holmes pointedly ignored the absence of enthusiasm.

"Good, you will need to wear those outfits one more time." Moving quickly to avoid objection, he turned to Lucinda Wiggins who was waiting hopefully for a role in the unfolding drama.

"Mrs. Wiggins, it appears you did not attract the attention of the police at the last march. Can I say that, in spite of your considerable contribution, you would be unknown to the authorities?" There was a broad smile and vigorous nod from Lucinda Wiggins.

"Very good. I have it in mind that you will be matched with Miss Kenney on the back fringe of the left side of the marchers. It is our, that is, it is my judgement that the rock-throwers will be on the back fringe of the march to avoid detection and to get quickly away. The two sets of eyes you and Miss Kenney can provide should enable us to identify and call attention to the rock-throwers when they appear as I believe they will." Lucinda's smile broadened with Holmes's assurance that she would be a part of whatever was to happen the next day.

"Miss Pankhurst, I mean for you to play the same role as your colleague, but you'll be stationed on the right side of the march. Again, you will be at the back fringe, there to be paired with Miss Lestrade if agreeable to her and to the inspector and Mrs. Lestrade."

The plan was instantly agreeable to Millicent, her only regret, unspoken, was that she could think of no reason to be in disguise for her performance. The inspector was loathe to disappoint his daughter, and so, armed with his own ideas about maintaining her safety, he agreed, after a nod from Mrs. Lestrade, to his daughter's participation. Mrs. Lestrade's only regret, unstated, was that there was no role for her in the plan Holmes presented.

Holmes had succeeded in gaining the cooperation of four of the participants in the action planned; he now had arrived at the point of gaining the cooperation of the two additional participants essential to the plan's success—the two least likely to be agreeable to the actions proposed. He swallowed hard and began.

"You understand we will need corroborating witnesses for the women's statements." His audience rewarded his observation with cautious nods and blank stares.

"Witnesses who are not themselves known to be associated with the votes for women movement but are willing this once to appear to be part of the movement by making themselves indistinguishable from other participants in the march—going undercover so to speak—and thereby able to give unbiased eye-witness accounts of any wrong-doing." This time when Holmes looked around there were only blank stares, his audience waiting to learn where Holmes intended taking them. Holmes, meanwhile, was thinking how much easier it had all seemed when he was rehearsing his talk with a far more responsive Watson. Regardless, it was now time to satisfy their understandable curiosity.

"We must now think in terms of the witnesses we will want to summon to corroborate the reports that Miss Pankhurst and Miss Kenney will provide. While we will have Mrs. Wiggins and Miss Lestrade, I think we can all agree that in this day and time—and given that votes for women is the issue—the persons who can make the best witnesses on their behalf will be men unaffiliated with the movement." Holmes looked his most serious as he now scanned his audience. Again, he found a wary attentiveness. He continued with what he knew to be the most contentious part of the plan developed at 221B a little more than twelve hours before.

"Within the ranks of possible male witnesses, it seems likely that the best we could hope for would be a member of the Metropolitan Police together with someone he affirms to be acting under his direction. A police officer or his designee is certain to be believed when he reports a crime and cites the wrongdoer. That is why I am asking Constable Lestrade to lend himself to the effort to identify and punish the people responsible for window-breaking. At the same time, as we have discussed, to guarantee the success of our efforts, it will be necessary that all involved be indistinguishable from the suffragette marchers such that the rock-throwers are not deterred from revealing themselves."

For a moment, Holmes felt a massive sense of relief. The worst of it was finally out there. But relief lasted only a moment. There was first the sound of a massive groan as if the room itself had difficulty incorporating what had just been spoken. It was immediately followed by a voice made up of equal parts of incredulity and outrage.

"You can't be serious, Mr. Holmes." Noah Lestrade looked to the deadly serious Sherlock Holmes. "I would be the laughing-stock of the station. And that's only if your crazy scheme worked. If it didn't work, I could never live down the disgrace. I could even lose my job. I can't do it; I won't do it."

There was a single deep nod of agreement from the senior Lestrade, everyone else waited spellbound for Holmes's response. In fact, in the last evening's practice, Noah Lestrade's response had been seen as inevitable and a reply to it had been devised for Holmes's delivery.

"First, it should be understood that none of our disguised marchers will attract attention unless the rock-throwers reappear. If they reappear and are recognized by Miss Pankhurst, she will so inform Miss Lestrade who will go to alert Constable Lestrade that the rock-throwers have been spotted. She will then go on to involve officers assigned to policing the march about the rock-throwers. Constable Lestrade, meanwhile, will go to where Miss Pankhurst can point out the rock-throwers allowing him to monitor their movements, without himself being identified, until the officers alerted by Miss Lestrade arrive on the scene. At that time, Misses Pankhurst and Lestrade can describe the situation to the officers while Constable Lestrade slips away so as to continue to go unidentified. Of course, the same procedures will be followed by Miss Kenney and Mrs. Wiggins and Mr. Wiggins if Miss Kenney is the first to spot the rock-throwers."

Studying his audience, as he had learned to do from his years with Mrs. Hudson, he was relieved to see foreheads no longer creased in consternation, eyes no longer in a tight squint and mouths no longer set in tight lines. At least that was the case with everyone other than Noah Lestrade and Thomas Wiggins. Indeed, Wiggins opened his mouth to demur but caught sight of Lucinda's proud smile. He closed his mouth and adopted a weak smile of his own.

Noah Lestrade, too, was about to voice misgivings when he found himself challenged with words much as Wiggins had had to contend with a smile. Both men were fated to lose the argument each had framed for rejecting Holmes's proposal while winning the greater prize that lay behind a proud smile and a single sentence unexpectedly making use of a Christian name.

"That sounds like a reasonable plan, Noah, don't you think?"

The questioner surprised several, the personal nature of the question surprised all. Christabel Pankhurst took no notice of the reaction of others. Noah Lestrade, on the other hand, reddened somewhat and the hint of a smile lasted just long enough to dispel all evidence of his earlier skepticism.

"It does sound reasonable," Noah tentatively agreed, before seeking guidance from a source of instruction he more typically felt he'd outgrown. "What do you think, Dad?"

Inspector Lestrade had been considering Holmes's proposal well in advance of his son's unexpected request. Like his son and Wiggins, his response was shaped by the influence of a woman—indeed, two women, as out of the corner of his eye, he could see that both his wife and daughter were showing a keen interest in his response to his son.

"I can say this, Noah, Mr. Holmes's plan is clearly not without risk; however, I cannot recall a time in our work together that a proposal of his, no matter the risk, met with any but success. It has almost seemed as if Mr. Holmes has access to some higher power that allows for a greater intelligence than is possessed by mortal man. Nonetheless, the risk remains and, it must be said, it's been some time since Mr. Holmes and I carried out an investigation together."

For his part, Holmes could not recall an instance at any time in which he and Lestrade had carried out an investigation together. He thought it unwise, however, to correct Lestrade at that moment.

Noah, meanwhile, whatever his misgivings, had reached a highly predictable decision. "I'll do it, Mr. Holmes, and hope for the best. It seems essential to our seeing justice done."

The inspector smiled, his mother beamed, Millicent applauded, while the woman on whom his eyes fell looked to him with an admiration that made clear his choice was inspired.

The next day shown bright and sunny with only the smallest nip in the air to remind everyone that fall had arrived. It was enough to induce most marchers to dress in traveling suits whose long skirts and jackets guaranteed comfort regardless of the elements. Some women, more willing to brave whatever elements awaited, disdained jackets, instead flaunting shirts and ties to make clear the equality with men they felt, and they demanded.

In accord with plans agreed to the day before, two stout women took positions well to the back and at opposite edges of the vast crowd of women and a handful of men. Each of the buxom women was soon joined by a young woman, their only communication an exchange of glances as they stood together while seeming apart. Minutes later, two more marchers joined the crowd, one from the right and one from the left, each of them within sight and shouting distance of the women who had entered earlier on their side. Unlike those earlier entrants, these marchers appeared to be having some difficulty maneuvering their way through the throng of marchers, causing more than one marcher to express the hope that the newcomer was sober. Others, of a more charitable bent, hoped the women had not risen from a sick bed to which they appeared destined to return. None attributed the marchers' difficulties to the struggle each was having with the adoption of a dramatically new identity and matching outfit. As the march got underway, concerns about anything other than the movement and its objective were quickly dismissed. At that point, those who had inconspicuously joined the march at its fringes now fell inconspicuously to its back.

Leading the march was the Women's Fife and Drum Band, the band members dressed in uniforms of purple, green and white, the colors of the Women's Social and Political Union, which had become the dominant organization in the struggle to get women the vote. Beyond the band, in the first rows of marchers in recognition of their contribution to the movement, were Sylvia Pankhurst, Christabel's younger sister, Millicent Fawcett, Minnie Baldock, Mary Phillips, and Flora Drummond. Behind them came nearly a thousand women carrying banners that demanded "Votes for Women" in lettering of a size that would not cause eye strain for any onlooker. The plan was to start at the Embankment in the area of Waterloo Road and to proceed along Victoria Embankment, to assemble finally at Parliament Square, there to hear speeches and to make clear their numbers and their commitment lest any in government doubt either.

Whatever may have been the concerns of its organizers or of the authorities assigned to police it, the march began and proceeded without incident. The fife and drum corps played tunes that were appropriately martial and the marchers set their faces to look appropriately militant. The onlookers they passed reflected the range of support for the movement and its lack. Two men stopped their heated conversation to give dismissive waves to the marchers, one of them supplementing his gesture with a shouted suggestion they return home to care for their husbands and children. Countering the male detractors, a small group of women stopped to give smiling applause to the marchers. They were briefly joined by a well-dressed young man who adopted both their smiles and applause before going on his solitary way. One woman, pushing a perambulator, stopped to gape, expressing neither approval or disapproval, only wondering at a site still novel even as it was becoming increasingly less so.

For their part, the women who had joined the march late and at its fringes, were well into the spirit of the march even as they remained alert for any sign of the rock-throwers they were seeking. Their well disguised escorts struggled to remain within earshot of the women they were surreptitiously accompanying.

The march continued on its peaceful way and seemed destined to reach Parliament Square without any apparent need for the highly visible police presence. It was then Christabel Pankhurst, recognized the two rock-throwing policemen responsible for hers and Annie Kenney's predicament. A word from her sent Millicent Lestrade on her way first to alert her brother to hurry to Miss Pankhurst's side, in so far as inexperience with his mode of dress allowed him to hurry, then to engage presumably more responsible policemen to come to the aid of what were presumably two women.

The two constables spotted could have been seen as assigned to keep the marchers contained on the Embankment lest they wander off to attack businesses on streets adjoining the marchers' route. There had been, however, no evidence of marchers straying from the parade route. Moreover, and more ominously, the constables' pockets appeared to be bulging with what Christabel took to be the remains of nearby roadwork. She pointed them out to a heavily breathing Noah Lestrade who had joined her finally, and both looked around for Millicent in the company, as they hoped, of a constable, and preferably two or more constables. What they could not know was that the constables she approached were convinced that Millicent was one of the troublemakers who, they had been warned, would try to get them to desert their posts in keeping with the master plan the parade's leaders were following.

As it became clear that Millicent would not be coming any time soon, and with the tail end of the march now passing Great George Street with its tempting array of windows in the recently constructed government buildings, it was apparent to Noah Lestrade that he would be forced to take the action he had dreaded all along. Mustering as much authority as he could manage in the wig and dress he wore, he demanded the two constables empty their pockets bulging with what he, too, took to be a ready supply of rocks.

Speaking in his normal voice, his baritone speech at first confused the two men, but only at first. In the next moment they jointly decided they were being confronted by one of the numerous unfeminine female troublemakers who were intent on disrupting their world. Accordingly, they warned Noah Lestrade to move on or be arrested. This left Noah in a quandary. If he maintained his false identity, he was bound to fail to hold the two men for questioning. If he revealed his true identity, and was able somehow to take the two men into custody, he could himself face charges of insubordination for undertaking an investigation without proper authorization. Moreover, given his current dress, any charges he sought to bring would very likely be dropped after first exciting brief hysterics in his fellow officers and superiors. In a best case scenario, he would, as he had earlier suggested, be retained on the force while remaining a source of continuing amusement until his retirement and likely beyond.

He was about to choose a lifetime of ignominy when a familiar voice made any such choice unnecessary. It occurred to him then that while the women looked back to keep him in sight, he had no reason to look back and had no idea who was behind him.

"I suggest you follow the advice you were just given. You may know me. I am Detective Inspector Lestrade, recently retired from Scotland Yard, and still very much concerned with seeing that law and order prevail. Now, I'll thank you to empty your pockets and state your names." Lestrade took a notepad and pencil from his pocket and held the pencil at shoulder level while awaiting the two constables' response. Seeing in the near distance a police sergeant and two constables, roused finally by his daughter, coming quickly in his direction, the inspector turned to the woman who was his son.

"You are now free to leave. Thank you for your assistance." Noah Lestrade also had a view of the fast approaching officers and left with a speed that very nearly caused him to run out from under his bonnet.

Lestrade turned his attention back to the two officers. "I have a proposal for you which I suggest you take, or you will be facing what I guarantee will be a lengthy time in Newgate. I will personally see to that. First, you will empty your pockets of the stones you are carrying. Second, you will admit to now being uncertain about claims made earlier regarding the identification of certain women as rock-throwers. Having made that mistake in the heat of the moment, you wish to correct the record as regards the arrests made. And third, in light of the needs of the Empire and to atone for your errors, you are volunteering to serve in the constabulary now being created for the territory of Nyasaland on the African continent."

The two men looked to each other, their jaws dropping but making no reply. Lestrade would have none of it. "Your names and your pockets."

"Charles Dickson."

"Alan Carter."

As they spoke, a small fusillade of rocks fell from their pockets.

"And you are agreed to volunteer for Nyasaland? Or would you rather spend the next year or so greeting old acquaintances in Newgate Prison?"

Agreement was grudging and given at a little above a whisper, but met Lestrade's demand for speed.

There followed silence until the sergeant and two constables came finally within earshot. The sergeant's greeting convinced Dickson and Carter of the wisdom of their decision.

"Detective Inspector, sir, it's good to see you again. You may not remember me. I'm Sergeant Paul Heath and these are Constables Leaphart and Branch."

"Of course, I remember you, Sergeant. You were most helpful in our capturing the Cotswold kidnappers as the scribblers called them. I'm afraid I don't know these officers however."

"No, you wouldn't, sir. They're new since you left. But they know you, sir. You left your mark on the force and there's still talk about you, sir. All of it more than good, I assure you."

"Well, thank you, Sergeant. That's very kind. And as you see, Dickson and Carter have collected a goodly number of stones in a sort of street cleaning effort. There's also some issues they wish to clear up at the station so I'll let you get on with your work. I'll just drop back to the station later to see that everything went off alright. Very good seeing you again Sergeant, and nice to meet you, Constable Leaphart, Constable Branch, good luck to you both."

There were nods all around and the word "sir" was spoken with some frequency, sometimes with marked respect, sometimes with marked resignation. It was all the same to Lestrade who'd done what he had promised Mrs. Lestrade he would do.

That night there was a small party at the Lestrades's terraced home to celebrate the dropping of charges against Christabel Pankhurst and Annie Kenney, which the inspector had confirmed in his promised visit to the police station. Thomas and Lucinda Wiggins were, of course, invited and became the subject of several toasts, each made with cups of tea held aloft. Noah Lestrade made up his mind to enter into the spirit of things, only to find that entering into that spirit was far less difficult than he expected as he accepted thanks for a contribution that only those present would ever know about. Holmes won easy approval for extending a party invitation to Mrs. Hudson. It came, however, with the stipulation that she be asked to please bring scones for ten people. She brought scones for twenty and saw them disappear with impressive speed. Only Watson was unable to attend. Seeing the melancholy state into which he had fallen with his colleagues leaving to celebrate the exoneration of others, Mrs. Hudson felt obliged to assure him an equally grand party was not far off for him. She spoke with such certainty that Watson found his spirits improbably raised while Mrs. Hudson felt renewed pressure for making good on her hunch.

After completing several renditions of *For He's a Jolly Good Fellow*, each rendition modified to fit the gender of the person being celebrated as jolly good, the party evolved into a series of small groups, one of Holmes and Lestrade reminiscing about cases with Thomas Wiggins an avid listener; another with Annie Kenney holding forth for the benefit of Lucinda Wiggins and Millicent Lestrade a description of activities planned and completed by the suffragettes. Meanwhile, Mrs. Lestrade gratefully accepted Mrs. Hudson's assistance clearing dishes, and washing and drying them while they speculated on when women might get the vote, both believing in its inevitability, and what victories might lay beyond that in gaining increased opportunities for women.

Two people absented themselves from the activities inside the Lestrade home. Once again claiming a need to get some air, Christabel Pankhurst and Noah Lestrade went for a walk together. They spoke first of the day's activities, each expressing admiration for the actions of the other. Talk of the day's events quickly gave way to talk about themselves, and how much each had learned in the last few days. For her part, Christabel acknowledged she would never look at a policeman in quite the same way again and Noah said the same about women in the movement. Each went on to express appreciation for having known the other, while stopping short of sharing how each felt about the other. Both knew, but neither would say, that this would be their last walk together, even as both knew, but dared not admit, each was destined to carry in memory a fond recollection of the other. They had become friends, in the process overcoming barriers of beliefs and social position. Together, they had come a long way, but they could go no farther.

Chapter 9.
Where Is Watson?

If the night brought celebration, the following day returned the Baker Street trio to the challenge of unfinished business. Constable Chase brought them news of the latest complication in their effort to conduct that business.

Although the early hour meant the street was nearly bare for other than costermongers positioning themselves for the day's sales, the constable's promised revelation led to his quick removal from that street and entry into 221B. "There's something I just heard that you should know but you never heard it from me."

In the privacy of Mrs. Hudson's parlor, after first rejecting the offer of tea while accepting the offer of a scone, the constable shared the news he'd heard. "You should expect a visit from the Yard." Unable to resist the temptation of the treat he held, he bit off a piece and chewed it thoroughly before elaborating on his somewhat disturbing message.

"I got called in to ask if I'd seen anything suspicious. I told them things looked the same as always except for maybe Thomas Wiggins being around but I explained how he used to be a page here, and how even before that Mr. Holmes used him and some of the other lads to get him information on some of his cases. I said how all of that took the surprise out of my seeing Mr. Wiggins here. I told them Mr. Holmes was likely doing things with Mr. Wiggins to prove Dr. Watson didn't kill anybody—which I told the people from the Yard was something I agreed with—I mean about Dr. Watson not killing anybody. That's when they told me they weren't interested in what I believed, just in what I saw. I told them I hadn't seen any sign of Dr. Watson, and they told me they'd take it from there, but that it might prove useful for me to stay close by Baker Street this afternoon. And that's where it was left. At least that's when they told me they had work to do and they were sure I did too. I just think you should know, Mrs. Hudson, in case Mr. Holmes is working on a case he wants to keep hush hush, or there's things you want to keep private or put someplace out of the way because they'll just go through like Billy be damned." With an embarrassed grin, and a "pardon my language, Mrs. Hudson," Constable Chase prepared to take his leave.

Before he could return to the London streets, Mrs. Hudson managed to stuff one more scone in his pocket and to thank him at length for his visit, all the while wondering whether his words and action reflected the naivete about the activities at Baker Street that he professed, or provided the cover for a far greater sophistication about those activities than she had ever suspected. She gave it up finally, deciding it was a puzzle to be worked out another day. For now, there was a need to deliver Watson elsewhere as the lumber room was sure to prove unsatisfactory in the event of a thorough search. Lestrade's home was clearly out. Enough had already been done to jeopardize Inspector Lestrade's reputation and Constable Lestrade's career. There was also the Wiggins's home, but the police already knew of Wiggins's alliance with Mr. Holmes and would undoubtedly be following up with Thomas and Lucinda as part of this latest search. Indeed, Thomas and Lucinda were the only people, outside of Mr. Holmes and herself, who knew where Dr. Watson was— apart from Thomas's one-time colleagues who, she felt reasonably certain, would have reason to limit their interactions with the police—and denying knowledge of people and things to the police would not be a novelty for them or for Thomas and was likely a skill he had communicated to Lucinda. She considered and promptly dismissed a trip to Sussex Downs and Mr. Holmes's cottage. She simply couldn't be sure there would be the time for it.

All things considered, she believed the best, if not the only strategy available was hiding in plain sight, making use of Mr. Holmes's play-acting materials and hoping those materials would provide the concealment she did not feel they could ask others to provide. There was now only Dr. Watson to be convinced of the need to be disguised and to become someone he wasn't.

Holmes embraced the task of Watson's transformation with unconcealed relish. Watson was significantly less enthused. For the second time within a week, Watson's moustache became a major bone of contention. Holmes viewed its removal as critical to the close inspection to which Watson would be subjected. Watson argued that moustaches were far too common to be viewed as significant to anyone's identification.

Watching the byplay of her two colleagues, Mrs. Hudson was becoming increasingly concerned. It was past mid-morning. Preparations for their likely afternoon visit should be concluding, but neither man was yet ready to accept the other's thinking. The truth, as she knew it, was that Holmes welcomed any opportunity to engage in what he called "camouflaging oneself" and she called "dress-up." Watson viewed it as a device that was sometimes necessary, as with his return to Baker Street, but preferred to engage in it sparingly and with as little change in appearance as possible. The truth was he thought it was fine for Holmes, whose true calling was the stage anyway; for himself, it was a subterfuge that made him uncomfortable in its adoption and barely competent in its performance.

Knowing their differing views and watching those differences play out in her parlor, Mrs. Hudson was of the opinion that a different strategy was called for and she believed she had one. Calling a halt to a heated discussion having to do with the utility of a false beard and its most appropriate size, shape and coloring, she broached her idea for dealing with the afternoon's visitors and their search for Dr. Watson. It was embraced instantly and enthusiastically by the doctor and slowly and reluctantly by Holmes, but, in the end, both men were ready to play their parts and the next phase in the continuing effort to keep Watson from the gallows was begun.

The two men from Scotland Yard arrived at a little past two. The two men identified themselves by last names, Buchanon and Laskey, neither of which were familiar to either Mrs. Hudson or Holmes who had come downstairs from the sitting room to meet them. They, on the other hand, did know Holmes and directed a somewhat embarrassed explanation of their visit to him.

"We mean to be as little disruptive of your life as possible, but we have orders to search your home top to bottom looking for a suspected felon thought to be in the area. I believe you both know a John Watson who was resident here at one time." With the smallest of nods both Mrs. Hudson and Holmes admitted to knowledge of the miscreant.

The man named Buchanon, who had looked uncomfortable from the start, now voiced one cause for his discomfort. "It appears we may be here at a bad time, and I apologize for that, ma'am. I believe we may be interrupting some business of yours, judging by the delivery van that's tied up outside. It looks to belong to a Lewis and Sons."

"You are indeed interrupting business, officer. And it's actually Lewin not Lewis, and it's not really sons, It's more like son-in-law, which is me. Thomas Wiggins, printer." The voice preceded the body that emerged from Mrs. Hudson's parlor and set a tone of businesslike command. "The landlady, Mrs. Hudson, and me were just going over the designs for flyers and signs to advertise the availability of rooms to let in her lodgings house. There's quite a demand for housing and Mrs. Hudson has wisely decided to work with experienced sign makers, which is to say Mr. Lewin and me, to get the word out about her very attractive rooms. I don't suppose either of you gentlemen is in the market for rooms or know anyone who is?"

Buchanon and Laskey shook their heads in unison. "No, thank you, Mr. Lewin, you might just as well get back to your business and we'll try not to disturb you anymore than is necessary."

Wiggins nodded his appreciation of their concern, and ignoring being misnamed, he handed each of them a business card "just in case you have a printing need in the future, or know someone who does." Wiggins then returned to Mrs. Hudson's parlor and the sample signs he had spread across her table. Mrs. Hudson joined him after offering her uninvited guests tea and receiving their expected rejection. Holmes, meanwhile, joined the search for Watson to the obvious displeasure of the men from Scotland Yard.

Unsurprisingly, the men from the Yard found no trace of John Watson. After three-quarters of an hour of checks, double-checks and some triple-checks, they pronounced themselves satisfied that wherever Dr. Watson was, it was not inside Mrs. Hudson's lodgings. They exited with declarations of apology for disturbing people and a call from Wiggins to remember Lewin and Wiggins for any printing need, and got back in the coach they had parked just behind the delivery van. It was as close as they would come to finding Watson.

Earlier in the day, in response to a telephone call from Holmes, Wiggins had arrived with the delivery van that was used to convey larger signs or print jobs. When the streets were clear, Watson was set in the van with the door just enough ajar to allow air in. Contemplating a lengthy period in the dark, Watson brought with him a copy of *Lancet* and a device Watson had read of, invented by a David Misell, that allowed a person to cast a beam of light in an otherwise dark enclosure. Making himself as comfortable as his somewhat cramped quarters allowed, he would wait there with his journal until the two detectives completed their search for him. With the police coach safely in the distance, a somewhat stiff Watson was helped from the van to return to the comparative comfort of the 221B lumber room. As she held the door for his return, Mrs. Hudson thought she saw Constable Chase crossing the roadway near the end of the street, but it was a long way off and she only caught a glimpse of the constable, if it was the constable.

They reassembled in Mrs. Hudson's parlor where they watched silently as Wiggins slowly gathered up the mock signs and materials he had brought to support the small deceit played out for the benefit of the inspectors. Before he left there was an exchange of congratulations, most of them heaped on Wiggins, but more than enough to allow for a sharing amongst all of them.

Chapter 10.
Digging Up New Evidence

With Wiggins gone back to boast to Lucinda of his accomplishments, Mrs. Hudson thought it time to take the next step in establishing Dr. Watson's innocence. It was obvious the authorities had stepped up their efforts to locate and ultimately to punish Dr. Watson. She and Mr. Holmes would need to step up their efforts to establish his innocence. It called for another meeting with her colleagues around the kitchen table and the enlistment of assistance from an unlikely source.

"It is time, one could say past time for us to identify the person responsible for the death of Reginald Miles and put an end to Dr. Watson 'avin' to stay in 'idin', and Mr. 'Olmes and me 'avin' to pretend we've no idea where 'e might be." Two emphatic nods indicated her feelings were shared by the two people she had named. Her next words led to the same people's withholding of support pending clarification.

"Mr. 'Olmes, it's my understandin' that you left Mr. Garfoyle with' im thinkin' 'e still owes you one more favor. Is that correct?"

"I suppose that's the case. But surely we don't want to approach Garfoyle for another favor. You do understand that he is quite disreputable. He appears to manage some number of illegal gambling operations in London, lends money at what I'm certain are exorbitant rates and I don't know, or want to know what all else. Frankly, it was a bit harrowing dealing with him earlier and I wouldn't relish getting involved with him again. I trust you're not proposing we join forces in any way with someone of his like."

It was, as Holmes soon learned, exactly what Mrs. Hudson was proposing. Moreover, she was proposing that

Holmes see Garfoyle as soon as possible in as much as the action she saw as necessary was to be conducted between 2 AM and 4 AM that evening, although it might be stretched to 4:30 if they encountered difficulty. With great reluctance Holmes admitted he had memorized Garfoyle's address.

As it turned out, Garfoyle was no more pleased with the task Holmes presented than Holmes was in presenting it. However, as he said several times in the course of their conversation, "a promise is a promise," and he would not welsh on his promise. He did not, however, offer Holmes either tea or crumpets during the short time he gave him. Nonetheless, the following morning, exactly as Holmes had requested, the body of Reginald Miles lay across the examining table in the coroner's office, two notes pinned to his jacket. One read: "body of R Miles delivered for autopsy as requested." The second read: "ask Sherlock Holmes to be present at autopsy." The final act of the evening was an anonymous call to the coroner's home urging his immediate return to his office.

On his arrival, the coroner looked to his uninvited guest on the examining table, read the less than explanatory notes, and made two calls. He wakened his assistant from a sound sleep to tell him his presence was required, and he wakened the detective inspector on duty from a fitful sleep to tell him his presence was requested. He told the inspector of Sherlock Holmes's involvement and the wish that he be contacted. The inspector said he would make certain to contact Holmes. It did not sound to the coroner as if it would be a friendly invitation. Indeed, the detective inspector decided he would not ask Holmes to appear at the coroner's office, he would demand his presence and he sent two constables in a police wagon to enforce that demand with perhaps the added benefit of embarrassing Holmes in front of any neighbors the police van happened to awaken.

Holmes had, in fact, received a telephone call at 4:30AM, claiming anonymity, while sounding a great deal like Garfoyle, who reported the body had been delivered as asked, then hung up without waiting for a response. When the police wagon arrived, Holmes was outside 221B waiting for it. Moreover, whatever the inspector's hopes, Holmes's neighbors were far too accustomed to the eccentricities occurring with some regularity at 221B to be put off by a police wagon whatever the hour of its arrival.

The several years in which he'd turned his attention from criminal investigation to beekeeping had taken a toll on Holmes's knowledge of the members of the Metropolitan Police. The detective inspector to whom he was delivered at the coroner's office barely introduced himself with a name Holmes barely heard and quickly forgot. He did remember Dr. Dorsey, the coroner, and remembered him fondly as an ally on more than one occasion. He gave him a warm smile and nod while, for his part, Dorsey expressed his regret about Watson's situation and went so far as to wish Holmes well in his effort to exonerate the doctor. The pleasantries concluded as far as the inspector was concerned, there followed a series of questions to Holmes while the coroner, his assistant and Reginald Miles all maintained their silence.

"What is this all about, Mr. Holmes? Why has Reginald Miles's body been dug up and brought to the coroner?"

"I presume, there is someone who feels there may have been a jumping to conclusions and a belief that a thorough investigation is in order."

"Like friends of yours?"

"I can assure you the people who did this are not friends of mine although I, of course, applaud their belief in doing their civic duty, and I urge you to let Dr. Dorsey get on with doing his."

The inspector ignored Holmes's request, nor did he show any signs of relaxing the tight grimace he had worn since Holmes's entry. "Isn't this, in fact, your doing Mr. Holmes? Hasn't the body been brought here at your direction? And why should I feel any obligation to examine a body that's been exhumed illegally?"

"You should feel an obligation because you know an examination should have been made at the outset, and because, in a very short time, Reginald Miles's body will be discovered to be missing from its burial plot and members of the press will become involved in wanting to know why. When they discover that the body has been delivered to the coroner by persons unknown, they will start asking questions, and I suspect your answers will lead to more questions, perhaps ultimately to a government inquiry. There is, however, a simple way out of all this."

Holmes paused long enough to listen to the labored breathing that now accompanied the inspector's grimace. The overall effect made Holmes thankful the officers of the Yard did not carry guns.

"At this time there's only the four of us who know about Miles's empty grave so there's still time to act. I suggest you announce that the transporting of Reginald Miles's body to the coroner's office was undertaken at the Yard's behest and was purposely scheduled for a time when it would not create a public spectacle. You can say the Yard deemed it necessary to take this action to make certain nothing is overlooked in determining the cause of death and the person or persons responsible. In that regard, you might let the cemetery people know that you have Miles's body and will return it when the coroner has completed his work. With that in mind, it might be well for you to ask Dr. Dorsey to make his examination of Miles's body a priority." An affable smile was meant by Holmes to signal his willingness to let bygones be bygones and was seen by the inspector as

Holmes's self-satisfaction with having shown up Scotland Yard.

Nonetheless, as a policeman, he recognized the legitimacy of the concerns Holmes was expressing. He recognized, too, the importance of putting the word out before the scribblers got wind of an empty grave and the Yard, and more particularly the inspector, lost control of the story. Indeed, it was past time for him to take back that control. He recognized as well that, whatever his feelings about Holmes, others at the Yard had a very different view, including one other who was his supervisor. His curt response was meant to cover all bases.

"We'll take it from here, Mr. Holmes. I won't deny you've raised some useful issues and now I trust this will be the end of your meddling in Yard affairs. I'll leave you to have a brief visit with Dr. Dorsey, whom I believe you know from an earlier time. And Dr. Dorsey, it might be a good idea for you to make a brief examination of Miles just to show we've attended to every concern the most nitpicky meddler could raise."

Dorsey watched the door's closing behind the inspector. When he was satisfied it was done, he waited a few seconds more before asking his assistant to prepare the body for examination and Holmes to come to his office to talk.

As Holmes later explained to his colleagues, "To say Dorsey's office was cluttered would be like saying the Thames is a pleasant stream." The eyes went first to the skeleton dangling in one corner. Although half expected, its sight was jarring nonetheless. Between the skeleton and a small desk was a long table without chairs, its role solely to be the support for the stacks of paper covering it. Holmes had visited Dorsey in his office before. He knew that however haphazard the stacks appeared, Dorsey could locate any form, report or memorandum hidden within them in a matter of seconds. His desk continued the pattern established with the table. Papers took up the whole of it except for a small area in front of a desk chair of indeterminate age that appeared hazardous to occupy. The only chair other than the one behind the desk was similarly littered with papers Dorsey now set about relocating. As he did so, he shared with Holmes his reason for wanting to see him.

"Mr. Holmes, I didn't want to interrupt your discussion with the inspector, but you should know a Mr. Worthington came to see me on behalf of the dead man's family—anyway, Mr. Miles's son and sister. He had their signed statements asking that the body be released for burial so the family 'could put this whole sorry mess behind them.' That's just the way this Mr. Worthington described it—'a whole sorry mess.' Well, the Yard said they had their man so there appeared no reason not to release the body. Anyway, that's what I thought and the Yard agreed. Of course, if I'd known of your involvement, Mr. Holmes, I would have looked to do otherwise.

"You know you're still a hero to many of us, Mr. Holmes, and you shouldn't pay any attention to these young folk who think they know it all." With that, Dorsey jerked a thumb toward the door the inspector had exited a short time earlier. Holmes assured the coroner he knew better than to be put off by the inspector, then thanked him for his attention to Miles's body, no matter how late. "Indeed," he smiled benignly on both the coroner and his assistant as he withdrew a sheet of paper from his pocket, "you remind me, Doctor, there are some things to which I'd appreciate you and your colleague paying special attention."

The coroner took the paper Holmes offered and after his own careful study, handed it to his assistant. When he was done reading, both men gave enthusiastic nods to Holmes, affirming, without speaking, their intent to undertake all that Holmes was requesting.

159

Two hours later, with all of Mrs. Hudson's and Holmes's queries addressed, Holmes declared himself well satisfied and ready to take his leave. For his part, Dr. Dorsey expressed the pleasure of working with Holmes, his broad smile providing unmistakable support for his words. His assistant wore his own big grin in anticipation of later informing his wife, who frequently expressed her opinion that dead people were a bore, that he had spent the day with a very much alive Mr. Sherlock Holmes. There was a final shaking of hands with Dorsey saying he looked forward to their next meeting, and Holmes nodding and smiling but not reporting the same wish.

At 221B, in the familiar setting of Mrs. Hudson's kitchen table, Holmes shared the findings Dorsey had given him although without the coroner's excitement and surprise.

"We appear to have had it right, Mrs. Hudson. I believe we're ready to declare Watson fully exonerated and name the person responsible for Miles's death. When the coroner's findings were shown to the Yard, I was promised the opportunity to do exactly that as long as we act within the next two days to be sure we stay ahead of the dailies, and we make certain Detective Inspector Laskey is present and the Yard's contribution is noted." He smiled at the last but made no comment.

"That gives us very little time," Mrs. Hudson said ruefully, "I believe the best way to 'andle this is to get everybody together where we can establish Dr. Watson's innocence and reveal the guilty party."

"How do you propose to do that, Mrs. Hudson?" The question was posed by a newly rejuvenated Watson.

"We will 'ave another dinner party at Dr. Watson's 'ome tomorrow at seven sharp, this one without Dr. Watson but with Mr. 'Olmes who will be there along with Inspector Laskey to reveal what we've learned about the death of Mr.

Miles. So, Mr. 'Olmes will be in Dr. Watson's chair at the table, and we'll 'ave Inspector Laskey in a chair along the back wall facing Mr. Holmes where 'e can be called upon when it's appropriate. We'll also ask the Smythes to do their regular jobs. Mrs. Smythe will cook, and Mr. Smythe will serve, and the both of them will be there when Mr. 'Olmes tells what 'e knows—which will come before we eat so most everyone can enjoy their dinners later. Like always, Mr. 'Olmes, you'll take the floor to set out all that's been learned." She looked to her colleagues and, unsurprisingly, found them ready to play the last act in the drama they had taken on for themselves.

"We'll send each of them telegrams and 'ave the boy wait for a response. Mr. 'Olmes you'll get in touch with Inspector Laskey to invite 'im with the understandin' that you'll be sharin' all you know about Mr. Miles's death and that you'll be wantin' to give credit to the Yard for contributin' to the solution of the case. That way, too, if anybody claims not to be able to attend, we can ask the inspector to use 'is influence to get them to come. I'll call the Wiggins's to get them to make up the invitations and get them out real quick, and I'll pay a visit to the Smythes to arrange the dinner menu and talk about what they're to do. After all that's done, Mr. 'Olmes, you and I can talk about what you're gonna say at the dinner tomorrow night and maybe practice some of it in the time we 'ave.

As it turned out, only the Smythes and the Wigginses expressed dissatisfaction with the arrangements. The Smythes, believing themselves to be talking to a fellow servant who would be understanding of their dilemma, spoke of the time frame as far too short to prepare a dinner party. Mrs. Hudson was understanding of their dilemma, commiserated on the unreasonableness of their betters who had no appreciation of the work involved, and encouraged them "simply to do the best they could." She left the Smythes still feeling overwhelmed by their task but all the better for having been heard.

Lucinda and Thomas Wiggins informed Mrs. Hudson that, while they would certainly make up the invitations as a rush job, they would have liked to have had opportunity to be present when Mr. Holmes made his pronouncements.

Mrs. Hudson agreed with them whole-heartedly, describing it as a major oversight and, on behalf of Mr. 'Olmes, pledged that, as soon thereafter as possible, there would be a get-together at 221B to discuss all aspects of the case and properly celebrate its conclusion. She pledged as well that Mr. 'Olmes would see to it that appropriate credit was given to the Wigginses in the expected newspaper accounts. That promise, however, led the Wigginses to demur loudly and in unison. It seemed that Mr. Lewin, Lucinda's father and Thomas's boss, had, at best, limited knowledge of the involvement of his daughter and son-in-law in criminal investigation and campaigning for votes for women and would, they strongly believed, vehemently disapprove of their actions—especially Lucinda's actions. He would, she was certain, see her as "risking life and limb" for a cause he saw as frivolous. Thomas would fare little better, as he'd be seen as working for that same frivolous cause and doing so on company time. In the end, it was agreed that a later get-together with Dr. Watson and Mr. Holmes would be sufficient—provided, of course, the dinner party at Watson's home went well.

Chapter 11.
A Second Dinner Party

It began well enough in that none of the invited guests raised objection to attending a second dinner party in Watson's home, although several pointed out that the last dinner party had not gone well. All were curious about the news Holmes had to share and several wondered if Watson would be making an appearance in his own home.

As each guest arrived and was shown into Watson's parlor, Holmes found himself in the unfamiliar role of host. Moreover, he was host to people he had earlier treated as suspects in a murder investigation. And if that was not sufficiently off-putting, he had also to indicate and explain the presence of the rigidly correct Inspector Laskey who appeared intent on blending into a non-existent background, thereby causing his enigmatic figure to become instead the center of attention. It was a relief when Mr. Smythe invited everyone to take seats in the dining room, although it did not go unnoticed that he did not add the customary "dinner is served."

Holmes called for everyone to take the seats they had occupied at the earlier dinner party. He took Watson's chair while the chair last occupied by Reginald Miles was left conspicuously vacant. Holmes chose to stand behind Watson's chair, assuring himself a commanding view of the evening's dinner guests as well as his remaining the center of their attention. Indeed, the Smythes were little noticed when they entered the dining room and took chairs set against its back wall. Inspector Laskey continued to be of interest as he took one of two empty seats set along the back wall some distance from the Smythes, but less so as the guests became increasingly accustomed to his presence. Holmes first reintroduced himself, then reintroduced the inspector, taking the opportunity to briefly allude to the invaluable assistance provided by the inspector and the Yard.

Holmes's characterization of the Yard was readily accepted by the dinner guests who attributed their ignorance of the Yard's contribution as appropriate to the essential mystery of police work. The inspector remained his stolid self, silently accepting Holmes's description of the Yard's role while waiting to see what Holmes had up his sleeve.

The preliminaries disposed of, Holmes was ready to begin the analysis with which he hoped and expected to shock his audience. His single regret was that Watson was upstairs in a guest bedroom rather than downstairs where he could witness his performance and take proper notes for another of his little stories.

"First, let me thank you for accepting the invitations sent and adjusting your schedules to get here on what I know was short notice." His smile to the group went unreciprocated by any of its members. Instead, the soliloquy he planned was interrupted by a less than friendly question from Cyril Worthington.

"Mr. Holmes, I'm certain I speak for everyone in saying, first, I did not feel we had a choice as to whether or not to accept your invitation, as I believe the presence of Inspector Laskey makes clear. Second, since we have all been summoned to review Reggie's death one more time, I have to ask, is there anything new to go over? I'm sorry about your friend, but I have a life to get on with."

Worthington's first observation met with a good many grunts of agreement and affirming nods that set the stage for a near unanimity of grunts and nods in response to his second observation. Holmes decided his plan to edge gradually into his findings would need adjusting.

"In a word, Mr. Worthington, the answer is yes, there is important new information that has come to light which we felt (a nod to Inspector Laskey) it would be best to share with everyone at the same time to avoid rumors or misinterpretation." Holmes looked to a quiet but seemingly unchastened Worthington and plunged on.

"In every investigation it is customary to look at motive and opportunity. In that spirit, let us start with opportunity and explore who had opportunity to cause the death of Reginald Miles. It can be argued that Watson acted to create opportunity for poisoning Miles by setting out frosted dessert wine glasses rather than clear and later excusing himself to check on dinner while presumably all others were in his study. Watson would, of course, argue, not unreasonably I would think, that the frosted wine glasses are simply more attractive befitting the occasion and in the absence of the Smythes, it was necessary for him to make certain of the dinner."

"Let's not forget, Mr. Holmes, it would have been Dr. Watson who gave the Smythes the evening at leisure." Stanford Johnson gave a vigorous head shake in support of his own observation.

"And, being a doctor, he'd know his way around poisons," Worthington was not prepared to give up his role of naysayer quite yet, but he was willing to modify it somewhat. "I suppose the same can be said of Henry Clark, what with him being an apothecary."

Henry Clark was about to have a few choice words in defense of apothecaries everywhere, and especially in Watson's dining room, when Holmes interrupted the potential for an ugly exchange.

"The truth is nearly all of you had opportunity to poison Miles. Watson had set out the glasses, but nearly all of you, for one reason or another, left the study while Watson was showing his photographs. Indeed, only Edward and Alice Miles stayed in the study to support Watson and to fill in when he went briefly to the kitchen. Where Watson differs from all of you is with regard to motive. Others of you had a need to rid your lives of a man Mr. Worthington characterized as a 'leech,' in that he was a frequent visitor to some of you, practicing blackmail to pay his gambling debts. Still others stood to get that much closer to what promised to be a substantial inheritance. Watson, alone amongst you, was not getting blackmailed and stood to gain nothing."

"As you may not know, Mr. Holmes, he did say some terribly harsh things about Reginald Miles after Margaret's death." Alice Miles then made clear what the terribly harsh things were. "Most all of us heard him say he held Mr. Miles in some way partly responsible for her death."

"In the aftermath of his wife's passing, Watson did express his feelings at her passing and at Miles for being less supportive than he felt he should have been while Margaret was alive, and less caring than he should have been at her passing. I believe most all of you will agree those are not unfair characterizations of Miles's behavior generally and would prove particularly infuriating in association with the death of a loved one. Moreover, Margaret died some time ago. Is it likely that Watson would wait all this time before acting and then take action in front of witnesses? Mr. James, in somewhat similar circumstances, answered one part of the question for us, telling me, if I might," Holmes made a nod to James, then proceeded without waiting for his nod to be returned, "I wouldn't wait to exact revenge." Wilson James winced slightly but took no issue with Holmes's comment.

Stanford Johnson had been twisting in his seat and could contain himself no longer. "We know the problems with Reginald, Mr. Holmes, we've all had to live with them. I've said it before and I'll say it again, it's a wonder he lived this long without someone doing him in. And I think I speak for all of us in saying I appreciate what you're saying about Watson. I'd remind you it was the police who decided

Watson was the killer. They were supposed to be the experts and we just went along with it."

Inspector Laskey sat silently without even a muscle twitch through the whole of Stanford Johnon's critique. Indeed, were it not for his frequent eye blinks, one could have taken him for a candidate for Dr. Dorsey's examining table. In the ensuing silence Henry Clark made clear that he, for one, was not yet ready to release Watson from suspicion.

"Who's to say Watson isn't our killer? How do we know Watson didn't use his medical training to hurry along his wife's death so he could get her money, and maybe Reginald found that out somehow and was getting money from Watson same as he was doing with others?"

"Because after making Dr. Watson our chief suspect, we did a thorough investigation of his background and activities since his marriage." The speaker was the suddenly animated Inspector Laskey. "There is no question we were influenced by Mr. Miles's accusation as seemed appropriate. The last words of the victim should carry a special weight especially when combined with opportunity. Nonetheless, as new evidence came to light, a part of it… a good part of it … credited to Mr. Holmes, we were able to look elsewhere to make certain that at the end of the day we make the right call. In that regard we found no reason to believe Watson did anything other than support his wife in her illness and took pains to make certain the money she inherited from her father, although willed by her to Dr. Watson, was nonetheless kept separate from his own earnings and, indeed, has remained so up to the present."

"Well then, it seems to me time—past time, if anything—to unmask the murderer among us. If nothing else, I would like to get on with dinner." Worthington had hoped to lighten the mood with his remark, but unsurprisingly found the mood unchanged. He did, however, create a cascade of calls for the identification of "the murderer among us," the phrase now having been adopted by nearly all around the table with questioning looks directed to those who didn't take up the cry.

The moment had arrived for Holmes to rejoin the conversation and he did so with the bombshell he had been readying since the meeting had begun. "The inspector and I are in full and total agreement that the person responsible for Reginald Miles's death is not in this room."

Gasps of surprise were matched by open mouths and head shaking. With the recovery of speech, there were appeals from all sides for Holmes to explain himself. The appeals turned quickly to demands and the demands became ever more strident.

Holmes raised a hand to quiet the din. "I understand you want to know who then is responsible for the death of Reginald Miles and I assure you we will get to that in due time, but I want you to understand how the inspector and I arrived at that finding." There was a gradual quieting of voices replaced, in part, by the sounds of chairs creaking into changed positions with their owners' squirming. Holmes was satisfied his request had been met.

"There was something one of you said in the course of our questioning that I found to be particularly revealing. It involved a visit to Reginald Miles from Mr. Worthington after they had long since lost contact with each other."

"We didn't just lose contact, Mr. Holmes. I believe neither of us had any interest in seeing the other. I certainly had lost all interest in seeing Reggie. But you're right, he asked to see me and I agreed to do so as long as he wasn't asking for money."

"And the reason for his wish to see you wasn't, in fact, to ask you for money, but to ask if you had contact with the moneylenders he owed. I believe you called them 'loan sharks.'"

"And it's sharks they are. I'm sure the inspector can tell you. They're gangsters pure and simple and they're part of an organization that takes no prisoners—if you get my meaning." Worthington looked knowingly to the inspector and was rewarded with a single deep nod that served to impress everyone around the table with both the inspector and Worthington.

"And that was very informative, Mr. Worthington, but it was what you said later that I found particularly revealing."

Worthington's face was screwed in concentration as he tried to recall what he could possibly have said that could be construed as revealing. Holmes refreshed his memory.

"You said that, after you told him you couldn't help him in his dealings with the loan sharks, he told you not to worry that he had a way to work things out."

"That's right." His memory jogged, Worthington was prepared to be completely forthcoming. "'To get even' was what Reggie said, meaning to no longer be owing. But how was that revealing?"

"Very simply, it suggested a new line of inquiry—a line that made it necessary to conduct an autopsy. Fortunately, when I explained the situation to the Yard they agreed that an autopsy was needed. I take full responsibility for digging up Miles's body and having it brought to the coroner's office. I felt it necessary to act as speedily as possible and to draw as little attention to the exhuming of the body as possible. Through my work over the years, I had developed association with some people I could rely on to work through the night recovering Miles's body and having it delivered to Dr. Dorsey, the coroner. Dr. Dorsey was good enough to come to his office right away in spite of the early hour. I can tell you that his work confirmed our … that is to say, my and the inspector's hunch.

"Good morning, Dr. Watson, very good to see you." With all eyes fixed on Holmes, the newly exonerated Watson had come downstairs and entered at the back of the dining room to take the chair next to Inspector Laskey. He nodded an acknowledgment of Holmes's greeting and tried to force a smile for everyone else, but it came out equal parts grimace and smile. It, nonetheless, led to shame-faced looks of welcome by most and words of welcome by some. Holmes let the scene stand a moment before drawing attention back to himself.

"As I was saying, the coroner's report confirmed our conclusions. You will, I am certain, all recall the collision between Watson and Miles when Watson was refilling water glasses and Miles turned into him suddenly. The glass fell and broke into pieces which Miles insisted on picking up. As a result, Miles absorbed a deep cut on the palm of his right hand. And you may remember he refused medical attention, accepting only his daughter-in-law's assistance, which led ultimately to an exposed cut when the bandage she put on fell off."

"Through no fault of mine, Mr. Holmes," Alice Miles sought to make clear.

"Through absolutely no fault of yours, Mrs. Miles. But it turned out that the exposed cut was central to our understanding of how Reginald Miles died. At the coroner's examination, the gash showed as cherry red, which Dr. Dorsey said he'd only seen with people who'd developed what he called a 'cyanide rash.' I assume that is something with which you are familiar as well, Mr. Clark."

The apothecary blinked a "yes, of course" before adding that he'd never seen such a case himself but understood that cyanide entering the body through a laceration could have that effect.

"Exactly. Thank you, Mr. Clark. I then asked Dr. Dorsey to examine thoroughly beneath the fingernails and to look inside the pockets of the clothes he was wearing which I had reason to believe were the same as he was wearing at the time of his death, given the understandable wish on the part of the family to put this terrible tragedy behind them by scheduling a quick burial. What the coroner found was that there were indeed cyanide grains beneath the fingernails on the right hand and grains in the right hand pocket of his trousers as well. In a word, what he found was proof that the poisoning of Reginald Miles was self-inflicted. Reginald Miles's murderer was Reginald Miles."

Holmes let his words hang in the air a moment before lending explanation to his remarkable statement.

"I believe Reginald Miles had come finally to a point in his life where he could see no way out of the problems he had created for himself. His out-of-control gambling had led him to borrow money from an organization run by an Everett Garfoyle and he saw no way to pay his debt. I can tell you from my involvement with the Garfoyle family in the course of an earlier investigation that they are not people to whom you would want to owe money. I believe Mr. Worthington can back me up on that although I don't believe from his own experience."

Worthington grunted acknowledgment, then sought to confirm Holmes's last statement before confirming his first. "Definitely not from my own experience, Mr. Holmes. Not in a million years—maybe more. Of course, I knew about Garfoyle and his moneylenders. Anybody who had the habit knew about Garfoyle. And if you knew about Garfoyle, you knew to stay away from him, him and his whole organization. Like I say I didn't know the man, but I did know people who borrowed from his lenders and couldn't pay back and not all of them are still around." As Worthington looked meaningfully to Holmes, his fellow guests looked meaningfully to him. Holmes was satisfied he now had confirmation of the desperate straits Miles was in and so had given his audience the basis for understanding his desperate solution.

"And we have reason to believe Reginald Miles knew he could be well on his way to joining the ranks of those who are no longer around. Worthington has told us there was no secret about the fate of those unable or unwilling to pay their debts. But Reginald Miles had a plan. He believed he had a way to cancel his debt to the moneylenders. Even better, he believed he had a way to get that money to his son and thereby make up for all the promises he had made and never fulfilled. In taking the poison he removed one of the two people between his son and his sister's inheritance. As you'll recall, and as Inspector Laskey has described, it was a point of honor for Watson that he would live on his own earnings and not make use of Margaret's money even though willed to him. That money could however only come to Miles's son in the event of Watson's death or his removal to prison. As we've seen, Miles made every effort to paint Watson as his adversary even unto his dying breath. All that was done for your benefit, of course. It made you all witnesses to the enmity between the two men, and more than that, his seeming fear of Watson's wrath, a fear that could then be seen as justified by the final scene in the drama he had concocted."

Holmes paused to give his audience time to get past their embarrassment at having been duped but found them instead waiting with rapt attention for his next revelation. He did not disappoint them.

"There was a problem of course. Dead men can't control the future. For the scheme to work, Miles needed a co-conspirator, someone he could rely on to set the scene for his dying, and take control of the situation after he was gone. More particularly, to point the finger at Watson at every turn. And who better to do that than the ultimate beneficiary of his sacrifice—the son for whom he could finally become a proper father.

Edward, when we questioned you, you told Mrs. Hudson and me that you had no knowledge of your father's will or his plans in that regard. Yet, you had on your table a stack of catalogues, the top one being a furniture catalogue from Thonet, a manufacturer of rather costly furniture based on the continent. For you to have received it, the catalogue would have had to have been requested well in advance of Watson's dinner party and your father's death. Which is to say, it would have to have been requested by you in anticipation of the money that would be coming to you as your father planned it and as he told you of his plans."

At the last, Edward Miles came nearly out of his chair in his rush to deny Holmes's charges. Alice, sitting beside him, tugged on a sleeve but he was having none of such a gentle form of restraint. "This is outrageous. Maybe this is the way you solve crimes, Mr. Holmes, by bullying people into some kind of confession, but I can tell you it's not going to work this time."

Edward's protestation was so strong, so seemingly heartfelt that Holmes wondered for the moment about Mrs. Hudson's judgment, but he pressed on as he knew he would be expected to do.

"That's all very well, Mr. Miles, but I would remind you that you were the one who called for a gathering in the study before dessert was served, allowing your father, among others, to leave the study and do what he had to do. And, of course, you yourself never left the study as you were at pains to let everyone know. Thus, in spite of a history of conflict with your father, you could never be accused of his murder. The conflict was, of course, dramatically on display at the dinner party—at least your side of it was. And I have to say the appearance of a continuing conflict between the two of you kept hidden from me that it was a ruse to keep me—and others—from seeing the collusion worked out between the two of you.

"There was, to be sure, further evidence of collusion between the two of you. You used the term 'loan sharks' to describe the people who have a hold on your father, yet this somewhat esoteric term was only otherwise shared with Mr. Worthington, and he was sworn to secrecy about those being the people to whom your father owed money. I feel certain Mr. Worthington maintained his secret." Holmes paused for all to see a long nod from Worthington. "In short, the only way you could know these things would be through a meeting with your father, undoubtedly the same meeting at which he shared with you his plan to make certain the hastening of your inheritance.

"One other detail had to be worked out. If your father was to be seen as having been murdered rather than as having committed suicide, it would be critical that any trace of cyanide on him or his clothes be eliminated. Barring that, it would be critical to get him in the ground as quickly as possible to avoid any possibility of such discovery. And so, you convinced your aunt and uncle of the urgency of getting these things behind you and employed Mr. Worthington to carry the message to the authorities. There being no apparent reason for an autopsy, the family's wishes were heeded."

Holmes paused long enough to allow the room to exhale before adding a last observation "I will only say this. You might have gotten away with this scheme but for one critical error. By implicating Watson in your little intrigue, you brought to bear forces that would not rest until the truth was found and our friend's innocence established."

Watson smiled his appreciation to Holmes, which all took to be for his action in hastening Watson's freedom, which it was in part, but was also for his recognition, however veiled, of their mentor and the true sage of Baker Street.

Edward Miles did not participate in the group's recognition of Holmes's work or the celebration of Watson's exoneration. Instead, for nearly the whole of Holmes's talk, he fairly shook with a fury that appeared to have taken over his body. When he spoke finally, it was in a voice thick with rage. "Mr. Holmes, I can only conclude that your years with only bees for company has rattled your brain. Your tale is laughable ... unbelievable. Your so-called observations couldn't stand the test of any real scrutiny." Miles paused in his search for additional words to express the indignation he claimed.

"To be fair, Edward," Worthington began, "your father did ask me to tell no one about his being in deep with the loan sharks, and I kept my word."

"What are you saying, Cyril?"

"I'm saying that Mr. Holmes has maybe got it right about your father at some point telling you about his owing people and you're just blotting out that conversation."

"And it was you who called for a break and suggested looking at Watson's photographs until things calmed down. I do remember that," Mrs. Clark added.

Alice Miles looked from Worthington to Mrs. Clark, then back to Worthington. Her looks made clear that if she could have her way, there would be two less people at the table and perhaps in the world. "You know this is terribly unfair. There's a reasonable explanation for all the things you're bringing up." A skeptical audience waited the reasonable explanation, but it was not to be.

"I don't feel that I, or Edward, owe you that. And I don't see any reason for us to continue participating in this nonsense." She stood at her place, and, by her action, pulled Edward from his seat as well. She was, Holmes noted, a far different woman than the one who had asked his advice about not appearing guilty of her father-in-law's death.

Alice sneered the rest of her response to Holmes and to the inspector, who wisely remained silent in as much as the discussion was about events of which he had no knowledge. "If you've reason to charge us with a crime, do so but you know you won't get very far. And even if what you think happened turned out to have really happened, there's been no laws broken, there's just the removal of a useless man who you think arranged his own death. There's not a person in this room who'll mourn his passing or find reason to speak his name six months from now."

"You may well be right, Mrs. Miles, but I wonder what you plan to do with the debts you will have inherited from your father-in-law and with a certain Mr. Garfoyle who is the person to whom those debts are owed. I guarantee he will not be as forgiving as the law may be. I suggest you prepare yourself for Mr. Garfoyle or, more likely, for one of his minions. Your father-in-law's scheme to keep the inheritance out of Garfoyle's hands cost him dearly, and we have yet to see with what success."

Looking to each other and to no one else in the room, Edward and Alice Miles strode quickly to the door of the dining room. Once at the threshold, Alice cast a last look of especial fury at Holmes and then was gone with only Mr. Smythe to bid her goodbye, his having hurried to open the front door before closing it behind the Mileses and fixing a small smile on his face upon doing so, after first making certain there was no one to see it.

The exchange with Edward and Alice Miles led to an anxious question from Stanford Johnson. "Mr. Holmes, should Violet and I take any precautions regarding this Garfoyle. It's no secret that Violet and I—well, really, Violet—will also get a substantial inheritance from her sister after Dr. Watson has passed. Meaning no harm to Dr. Watson (he gave a small nod and near smile in the direction of Watson), but might this Garfoyle person come to see us as well?"

Holmes waved a hand as if flicking away a small insect as he dismissed Johnson's concern. "I feel certain you and Mrs. Johnson have no reason to feel at risk. Your inheritance, which I trust will not come to you until a time well in the future, will come from your sister-in-law only passing through Dr. Watson. It has nothing to do with Reginald Miles and therefore Garfoyle will have no claim on it nor feel he has. He only seeks to get back what he feels Miles owes him."

On learning of their escape from danger, both Johnsons gave thanks to Holmes, Violet Johnson restating her thanks two more times with increasing feeling each time. For his part, with Watson again a free man, the death of Reginald Miles explained, and the role of Edward and Alice Miles described, Holmes found himself suddenly famished, and looking forward to the celebratory meal he felt himself to have earned. He called on Smythe to serve the food Mrs. Smythe had been warming and smiled an invitation for all to join him in the first course of Julienne soup that Smythe had already procured and was beginning to ladle into bowls. As it turned out, while all tried to adopt Holmes's upbeat mood and hearty appetite, it was only a few who were able to carry it off. Most gave up the pretense somewhere during the serving of guinea fowls or very shortly thereafter. Watson's relief was so great and his experience with the dramatics of Holmes's conclusion of cases so frequent that he, too, had no trouble digesting the entire meal. The consumption of wine went far more smoothly and accompanied a genial banter that lasted through the largely undigested dinner. Watson had Smythe uncork four bottles of his best claret, then found he had to send Smythe for a fifth bottle.

When the evening ended at last, it was on a note of relief as much as celebration. All agreed they had shared an experience, the like of which none would ever see again—or want to. There was a hanging back from leaving as they reprised incidents in that experience. When it came time finally to take their leave, they repeated last goodbyes and made promises to meet again at some uncertain time in some uncertain place. And then, the hall was again empty and the house once more belonged to Watson and Holmes, who experienced their own discomfort at taking leave of each other and so made their own uncertain promises of reunion, unaware that Mrs. Hudson had already scheduled their reunion in accord with her promise to Thomas and Lucinda Wiggins to pay proper attention to their role in the successful concluding of *The Adventure of the Gambler's Folly*, as Watson had named his latest story.

Chapter 12.
What Lies Ahead

As much as he was anxious to return to the Downs and the company of creatures that neither wagered or had concerns about inheritances, he had one stop to make before leaving London. For what he hoped was the last time, he traveled to the address he had memorized where he was again conducted by the bald young man to the barren office and the impressive figure of Everett Garfoyle. His host made no secret of his displeasure with the circumstances under which they were again meeting.

"I'm sure you'll forgive me for not getting up, bit of a problem with my legs. I congratulate you, Mr. Holmes. You have bested me and there's not many can say that. At any rate, I deal in wagers, among other things, and do not tolerate anyone who welshes on a bet. You made a bet that you could solve the problem of Reginald Miles's death in seven days to which I graciously added another three, extending it to ten. No matter, you cleared things up in less than the original seven. Now, my payment to you is Dr. Watson's freedom from any further obligation to me and my pledge that he will not be disturbed by me or any of my people.

"It's my understanding that an inheritance from Reginald Miles will only come available after Dr. Watson passes—which I now have every reason to believe will be a good long time in the future. Well, I'm a patient man, Mr. Holmes, and I'll wait for people to do the right thing when that time comes. In the meantime, those same people might be induced to make a good faith effort sometime soon just to show a cooperative spirit. But why am I telling you all this. It's no longer any of your concern unless you choose to get involved which would require a whole different wager between us, and I've never lost two wagers in a row to anyone."

The challenge provided no temptation and went unmet. Instead, Holmes excused himself explaining that he had a train to catch, without clarifying that the train in question was due the following day. The two men did not shake hands and Garfoyle still did not rise. The absence of hospitality did not go unnoticed by Holmes, nor did it cause him the least distress. Nonetheless, as he rejoined the London traffic, the air seemed suddenly less stifling, and his life seemed suddenly far freer.

Holmes's next summons to London and 221B Baker Street was a far cry from that which was brought by Wiggins at the start of what Watson had renamed *The Adventure of the Dubious Inheritance*. Mrs. Hudson had arranged the party she had promised Thomas and Lucinda Wiggins, and she made a point of informing Holmes that his presence was requested. Holmes correctly understood that "requested" was a less than subtle substitute for "expected." That was, in fact, entirely agreeable to Holmes who found himself somewhat surprisingly looking forward to seeing everyone again. He sent a reply telegram saying that he "would be happy to join them."

One week later found the Wigginses and the Baker Street trio in Mrs. Hudson's parlor, fortified with tea and scones, reminiscing about their latest achievement, and only after that subject had been exhausted, turning their attention to other triumphs in which Wiggins played a role. While all but Lucinda and Mrs. Huson participated in the discussion, none did so with greater enthusiasm than Thomas Wiggins. The junior partner at the recently renamed "Lewin and Wiggins, Custom Printers," informed all that his years as a page in the consulting detective agency were the best in his life until he met Lucinda, and the young couple looked to each other in a way that put Watson in mind of Margaret and Mrs. Hudson in mind of Tobias.

Wiggins asked Mrs. Hudson if he could show Lucinda where he used to live, knowing she had not seen the lumber room during her earlier time at 221B and wanting her to see the fine accommodations he'd been given. Mrs. Hudson readily agreed, only warning him it was a lot cleaner now than when he was living there. When the young couple was gone, the members of the Baker Street trio spent several minutes congratulating themselves on the work they had done launching Wiggins on a straight and narrow path. They were in further agreement that Lucinda was a lovely person who would keep him there.

Holmes then raised the question that had been on his mind since returning to London. "I've heard nothing about Edward and Alice Miles. To the best of your knowledge, has there been any change in their circumstances?"

Watson and Mrs. Hudson exchanged looks before the doctor responded to Holmes's question.

"I should tell you, Holmes, the Yard is being very secretive about where things stand with the Mileses. Inspector Laskey stopped by one time to express his and the Yard's gratitude for all that had been done, and specifically asked that his compliments be passed to you, Holmes, but he resisted our several inquiries about the Mileses. Even Lestrade was hesitant to share what he was able to learn from his contacts—or his contacts were hesitant to share any information with him. In any event, we know that everyone at the dinner party was questioned a second time by people from the Yard and that, 'after due consideration' as Lestrade put it, the decision was reached that there simply wasn't enough hard evidence to justify an arrest.

"What followed then, Holmes, was the Mileses' worst nightmare. Only a day or so later there was a terrible fire at the Mileses' house. It happened at night and the two of them escaped with their lives and not much more than that. There was some talk about an investigation because the fire seemed so suspicious, but the Mileses wanted no part of that. In fact, it was only days later they booked passage to Canada or America or maybe even Australia. Nobody knows where for sure, at least partly because before sailing they changed their names, maybe just for the voyage, but probably forever. It's caused quite a little excitement, I can tell you, what with people trying to figure out what's going on. According to Lestrade there's even been talk of contacting Sherlock Holmes." Holmes smiled at the near accolade before fluttering a hand to dispel any such thinking.

The Wigginses returned at that point, both of them smiling broadly although for somewhat different reasons. For Lucinda, the trip upstairs confirmed her belief she'd saved Tommy from a mean existence. For Thomas, the trip was a reminder that he'd given up a thrilling career in detection to be with the woman he loved.

As second cups of tea were poured and drunk, and the last of the scones disappeared from the serving tray, talk turned to the future each of them planned.

Wiggins spoke again of the pleasure he took and the success he was achieving in the trade Dr. Watson and Mrs. H had found for him.

Watson talked of his return to medicine and the satisfaction he felt in helping people through their most terrible crises. Nonetheless, he acknowledged that he missed their time together and the challenge of criminal investigation.

Holmes declared he felt no such loss in giving up detection, that he was perfectly content to continue with his beekeeping, that, indeed, he was writing a book about his experiences and discoveries.

Mrs. Hudson shared for the first time her thoughts of retirement, of giving up the lease on 221B and moving to

Brighten or Hove. Her revelation resulted in a chorus of protest, none more plaintive than Lucinda's.

"Mrs. Hudson, you can't do that. You mustn't do that."

Her concern brought forth all the maternal feeling Mrs. Hudon had never had cause to express before. "Why, what's the matter, child? Why should my plans concern you?"

Lucinda said nothing while Thomas Wiggens, sitting beside her, put his arm around her and took her hand. He spoke for her after he judged she was ready for him to do so. "You see, Mrs. H, Lucinda has a bun in the oven—so to speak, and you know I've no family. Lucinda's mother has passed and, of course, Mr. Lewin never remarried. Well, it's the kind of a situation where a man can do just so much, and it needs a woman to get through the … the whole of what's involved. In a word, Mrs. H, we were going to ask you if you would sort of help us out. In fact, we want you to be the baby's godmother."

Holmes and Watson had seldom seen an emotional Mrs. Hudson. They did now. Her eyes filled with tears and, just for a moment, her jaw seemed to tremble. The Wigginses now leaned toward her waiting her response while Holmes and Watson sat wide-eyed, anxious to hear her reply as well.

"Why, of course, I'll be 'ere for you. I'm 'onored that you'd ask me."

All relaxed instantly; all expected Mrs. Hudson's response, but all were nonetheless relieved to hear it.

The Wigginses had one last question. Again, it was Thomas who posed it. "Mrs. H, if it's a boy we'll name him Albert after Mr. Lewin, and if it's a girl we want to name her after you. Mrs. H, could you tell us your Christian name?"

Once again, the Wigginses leaned in to hear her response. This time they were joined by Holmes and Watson who didn't want to take any chance of missing the secret that had eluded them for more than a decade.

When her response came, it evoked a range of reactions. Watson's varied between the thoughtful look he wanted to show and the incredulous look he couldn't keep himself from showing. Holmes roared with laughter, unable or unwilling to contain himself in spite of Mrs. Hudson's stern look. Thomas and Lucinda Wiggins, meanwhile, looked to each other with something akin to apoplexy.

When, at last, Thomas found his voice, he spoke slowly and as authoritatively as he could manage. "Perhaps it would be best to use Hudson as a middle name."

And so it was that six months later, an announcement appeared in the morning dailies that read, in part, "On March 6, 1907, a baby girl, Mary Louise Hudson Wiggins was born to Lucinda and Thomas Wiggins. Attending the birth was Dr. John Watson. Helping to celebrate the happy event were Albert Lewin, the mother's father, Sherlock Holmes, the well known detective and a family friend, and Mrs. Hudson, the child's godmother. Mrs. Hudson's given name was not available at the time we went to press."

Epilogue

      Christabel Pankhurst and Annie Kennedy were good friends and leaders in the Women's Social and Political Union (WSPU), a militant women's rights organization focused on acquiring the vote for women. The militancy of the WSPU can be seen as a reaction to the lack of success of earlier and far more moderate attempts to gain rights for women. In that spirit, the WSPU, founded in 1903 by Emmeline Pankhurst and her daughters, Christabel and Sylvia, made use of such tactics as marches, heckling unfriendly speakers, rock-throwing and window breaking as well as hunger strikes in association with its members' frequent arrests. The reliance on such tactics, while making clear the refusal of women to respond passively to the limitations imposed by men, is nonetheless seen by many as creating less sympathy for the cause of women's rights and, ultimately, even delaying women's achieving the right to vote. In any event, World War 1 called a halt to the campaign for the vote even as it saw progress in achieving that goal. In 1918, Parliament passed legislation extending the vote to women over the age of 30 who could meet certain property qualifications. The same legislation gave the vote to all men over the age of 21 without property stipulations. It wasn't until ten years later, in 1928, that Parliament enacted legislation giving the vote to all women over the age of 21, making eligibility to vote equal for men and women.

      Christabel Pankhurst committed herself to a life of protest when, at the age of 25, she chose prison over a fine after being arrested for heckling a speaker from the Liberal Party. It was the first of several arrests for aggressive efforts on behalf of a woman's right to vote, sometimes leading to a hunger strike to help make better known the cause of voting rights. She gave leadership to those efforts even when in self-initiated exile in Paris to escape arrest in the United Kingdom through her editorship of *The Suffragette*, the organ of the movement. After propertied women were granted the right to vote and the right to stand for election in 1918, she ran for a seat in the House of Commons and was only narrowly defeated. She relocated to the United States in 1921, where she became an evangelistic spokesperson, lecturing and writing books on the Second Coming.

During a return to Britain in the 1930's, she was honored with an appointment as a Dame Commander of the Order of the British Empire "for public and social services." She spent the remainder of her life in the United States, passing away at the age of 77 in Los Angeles, leaving an adopted daughter, Betty, Christabel Pankhurst never having married.

Posthumously, a bust of Christabel Pankhurst has been set as a part of the Emmeline and Christabel Pankhurst Memorial in Victoria Tower Gardens. A plaque now marks her home in London, and her name and image are etched on the base of the statue of the suffragette, Millicent Fawcett, in Parliament Square.

Although a colleague and friend of Christabel Pankhurst, Annie Kenney came from a far different background. In accord with the practice of the day for the working class, Alice Kenney began working part-time in a cotton mill at the age of 10 while still in school. She was working full-time by age 13 and was no longer enrolled in school. Alice Kenney worked from six in the morning to six in the evening as a weaver's assistant with responsibility for fitting the bobbins and repairing thread that broke. In the course of that work, she lost a large part of one finger in a not uncommon industrial accident. She worked at the mill for fifteen years, furthering her education through self-study as best she could, and acting in support of the trade union movement to the extent possible. She was inspired by Christabel Pankhurst, the two became close after both were arrested and jailed as a consequence of their disruptive behavior at the Liberal Party meeting referenced above. The confrontational nature of her activities on behalf of votes for women led to frequent arrest, followed by hunger strikes and forced feedings. Her level of sacrifice was such that she was awarded a Hunger Strike Medal by the WSPU. Like Christabel Pankhurst, she elected to pause campaigning during World War 1 to support the domestic war effort. The WSPU publication, *The Suffragette*, argued that it was "a thousand times more the duty of the militant Suffragettes to fight the Kaiser for the sake of liberty than it was to fight anti-Suffragette Governments." She spent a part of the war speaking to gatherings of trade unionists to encourage their support for the war effort. Later, she published a body of her experiences in *The Sunday Post*, a weekly Scottish paper, that constitute a kind of memoirs.

In 1918, with victory in the battle for the vote now in sight, Annie Kenney allowed time for a personal life, marrying and giving birth to a son. She died consequent to a stroke at age 73.

Public recognition of her life and accomplishments came posthumously as was largely the case with Christabel Pankhurst. Her name, too, is etched on the base of the statue of Millicent Fawcett in Parliament Square. A plaque has been placed near to where she lived in Oldham, and a statue erected in front of the Old Town Hall in Oldham.

Like Detective Inspector Lestrade, Mrs. Hudson was not given a name by her creator, Arthur Conan Doyle. Both appear in about a dozen works by Sir Arthur and Lestrade fares a little better than Mrs. Hudson in that he is given a first initial—G. And while Mrs. Hudson's sole description refers to her "stately tread" (was the woman plump, dare we say, obese, or was she regal in her carriage?), the inspector is described at some length. Of course given the nature of that description—"a little sallow rat-faced, dark-eyed fellow"—fans of Lestrade, wherever they may be, might have wished for Mrs. Hudson's anonymity.

In any event, many of Sir Arthur's far more numerous fans have taken it upon themselves to add a corrective of sorts to our understanding of Mrs. Hudson's character, and have decreed that the woman's first name is Martha. They reason, if reason is the proper term, that Holmes somehow cajoled the woman who was his landlady to become his maid and housekeeper when he left Baker Street to take up beekeeping on Sussex Downs. That is, she would go from a position of collecting rents from boarders to working in a menial position for wages. Moreover, she would leave London to live in a remote village and become servant to a man described by Watson as "the very worst tenant in London."

In the years since Mrs. Hudson and Lestrade first came on the scene, both have become fixtures in the rich literature, and abundant movies, radio and television productions Sir Arthur could not have imagined. Neither has suffered for want of a given name and I for one see no need for any such corrective. Indeed, the very lack of description allows us to wonder about Mrs. Hudson and what really was occurring at 221B Baker Street.

www.ingramcontent.com/pod-product-compliance
Lightning Source LLC
Chambersburg PA
CBHW070019260626
47159CB00005B/1873